Just Another Day

JM Kearsley

TSL Publications

First published in Great Britain in 2024
By TSL Publications, Rickmansworth

ISBN: '978-1-917426-01-5

Cover & photographs courtesy of :
https://en.wikipedia.org/wiki/File:Siege_of_
Badajoz,_by_Richard_Caton_Woodville_Jr.jpg

Dedication

For John, Helen, Patrick and Claire

always my loyal supporters

Chapter 1

The panting dog raced for his life down the hillside, veering frantically around and between the thin shrubbery and rocky boulders. Paws slipped on pebbles and breath laboured in the animal's throat as he aimed for the imagined safety of the trees at the base of the hill. If he had been able to think in a rational way, he may have wondered why he seemed to spend most of his life running away from people. Why wouldn't they leave him alone to smell the abundant interesting aromas of the countryside, to hunt and scavenge for food, to sit and have a good scratch, to lie down and shelter in a rocky hollow when the sun was hot or rain beat down? Instead, here he was again, running away from those two-legged beasts who seemed intent on only doing him harm. He was nearly at the trees now. Maybe there he could lose his pursuers, but no. There they were, coming over the ridge of the hill – blue-coated soldiers shouting and slithering down the hillside after him, some whooping as they gave chase, making the life and death race into a game.

One man stopped and took aim with a musket. The shot rang out and a bullet ricocheted off a rock, causing the running dog to change direction. Stones rattled down the slope as the tired dog's paws tried to get a purchase on the loose ground. The soldier reloaded and tried again. This time he cheered when the bullet hit the dog in the leg, sending it tumbling down the hillside, howling with pain. The French infantrymen ran down the slope, praising their colleague for his good aim, and knowing that they would get a good dinner that night, the first for many days.

Suddenly one of the soldiers shouted an alarm, and they turned to see men approaching from the right. Even as the alarm sounded, a rifle banged and the man who had downed the dog screamed, falling backwards into a thorn bush, his stomach spurting blood. French cries mingled with the sound of rifle fire and the air clouded with puffs of acrid smoke as a patrol of British Light Infantry, taking cover now behind rocks and the stubby trees that grew near the base of the hill, continued to surround the startled Frenchmen with bullets.

Within a couple of minutes it was over. Taken by surprise, the French had hardly had time to retaliate and now only two were left alive of the five who had been chasing the dog. Captain Richard Camberwell, his sword loose in his hand, stood over the man in the thorn bush who was holding his stomach while blood seeped between his fingers.

"*S'il vous plais, m'sieur!*" pleaded the French soldier, the tears of pain rolling down his cheeks. Camberwell could see that he was young, little more than a boy, and his uniform was fairly clean and had no patches or rents. A new recruit. Despite the fact that this was the enemy, Richard Camberwell felt a surge of sympathy.

"Please!" said the youngster again, his face a contorted mask, speaking in English, thinking that the tall English captain did not understand him. "Shoot me."

Richard Camberwell glanced at the young man's wound. He had seen many such, and knew it was fatal, as did the French soldier. With a sad half smile, he sheathed his sword and took out a pistol. "May you be going to a better place," he said quietly and fired a bullet into the lad's brain.

"What do I do with this 'un, sir?" said a rough voice behind him. Camberwell turned to see stocky, ruddy-faced Sergeant Readman holding a Frenchman by the arm. The man's other arm was bleeding.

"Take him prisoner, Sergeant," said Camberwell, walking away from the dead man, the sympathy of a moment before lost in his more usual cold tones. "Wellington might find it interesting to question him." He raised his voice. "Tomkins! Binns! Trim! Take a walk up the hill! See if there are any more of the bastards about! Sims! You and Parker take a look to the south!"

"Sir!" came the reply as the men hurried to do his bidding

Camberwell turned at the sound of a low growl. A soldier was hunkered down near the large black dog, talking to it in a low voice. Camberwell smiled. Trust Will to leave the wounded Frenchmen to their fate and make straight for the dog. He watched as the youngster crept a little closer to the wounded animal, talking all the while, his hand out, palm upwards. There came another low rumble from the dog's throat but not as threatening this time. He was starting to sniff at Will's hand. This went on for some time, until the dog finally gave the hand a lick. Will put his other hand on the dog's head and stroked the matted fur gently, then teased some thorns out of the coat. Slowly his hand moved from the head to the bloody leg. The dog flinched and let out another growl. Will stroked and murmured again until the animal let his hands feel the injured limb.

"What's the damage, Will?" Camberwell asked, walking up to them, and provoking yet another growl from the dog. He stopped a prudent distance away.

"'E'll live, sir." Will tore a strip off his already ragged shirt and started to bind up the wound. "It's just a nick. Missed the bone." He stood up and Camberwell watched while he rummaged in his pouch for a piece of dried beef that he gave to the dog who ate it ravenously. The infantry captain smiled to himself. It was not surprising Will's sympathy was all for the dog. He was an outcast too, dragged up in the filthy London streets, fending for himself and often running away from the law. The dog eyed him silently, seeming to understand that here, for perhaps the first time in his life, was someone who meant him no harm but was trying to help. The hands that stroked his matted fur were gentle, the voice encouraging. The dog decided that here was a friend.

The small patrol quickly ascertained that the Frenchmen who had been chasing the dog had come from a much larger group who were camped some miles away. The smoke from their fires were plainly visible from the ridge. "They'll be wondering what happened to these bastards," said Camberwell. "Come on, lads. We'd best be getting back. There's too much smoke for it to be just a patrol. There aren't enough of us to see them off if they decide to investigate."

Will urged the dog onto his three good legs. "I 'opes yer not thinkin' o' bringin' that flea-ridden rat-bag back to camp, lad." Sergeant Readman eyed the dog critically. "We've got enough 'angers-on already. It's just another mouth ter feed. And look at 'im. Barely enough skin ter string two bones together!"

It was true. The dog's bones stuck out everywhere under patchy black hair. In fact, thought Will, the poor thing was so thin, it was a wonder he had managed to run away from the French at all and he would definitely not have made much of a meal. It was difficult to tell what sort of dog he was but there was a certain look of wolf about him, with the sharp nose and pricked up ears. The coat was matted and bald in places and there were sores on his back. But there was a spark in the animal's eye and the tongue that licked his hand was friendly. The dog's tail wagged and his whole demeanour said, "Please take me." Will was determined not to leave him behind. With an injured leg the animal would have no hope of evading anybody else who thought he would make a good supper. Will's beseeching blue eyes moved to Richard Camberwell.

"Please can I 'ave 'im, sir? 'E's got no chance if we leave 'im 'ere."

Richard Camberwell sighed. Will Tucker was his servant as well as one of the best soldiers in his Company, and he owed him a lot. He thought back to Ciudad Rodrigo, the besieged town they had won and left some weeks before. It was Will who had rescued his niece Megan from that bastard Lieutenant Deaville, and saved her from rape, at the same time revealing that the lieutenant had been a traitor, and for that he had had no reward except grudging praise from his superiors. Perhaps the dog would rectify the matter. Risking a tirade from Sergeant Readman he said, "Bring the dog along, Will. It probably doesn't deserve to become a Crapaud's dinner, though it would make a bloody poor one."

With Readman muttering under his breath about how he didn't know what the army was coming to when they had to rescue dogs now, the patrol moved off in the direction of the British camp. As they went, Camberwell thought of the smoke they had seen. No one had realised the enemy was so close. He wondered if the General would order an attack, or whether the two armies would pass each other by and not risk a confrontation

*

That evening, General Sir Arthur Wellesley, Viscount Wellington, commander of the British army in Spain, listened with interest to Camberwell's report, and watched as Richard Camberwell, senior captain of the 4th Kent Light Company, showed him the French army's approximate location on the map.

"You have no idea how many?" he asked, settling back in his chair. The tent canvas billowed slightly, sending wayward shadows back and forth from the flickering lanterns that lit the inside of the tent. A wind had sprung up and it was cold. Wellington could not remember when he had last been warm. Although it was March, the weather did not seem to be warming up at all. Winters in Spain's mountainous regions were not comfortable.

"No, sir," Camberwell answered. "We came straight back with the prisoner."

"Has he been interrogated yet?"

"Captain Shaw's doing that now, sir."

"Well, let me know what the outcome is. I need to know as much as possible about the French army's movements," said Wellington shortly, denoting, by his closer attention to the paperwork on the table before him, that the interview was over.

"Yes, sir." Camberwell saluted and left the tent, stepping out into the dusk.

Fires were being stoked for the evening meals – beef stew again he supposed. More watery gravy than meat. Despite the news that the enemy was less than ten miles away, Wellington had given no orders banning the lighting of fires. But then a camp this big would be hard to miss, and Camberwell thought that Marshall Marmont, the commander of Napoleon's northern army, would have his patrols out too and would know where the British were. After all, they had been here for nearly a week, waiting for Wellington and a portion of the army that had been left behind at Cuidad Roderigo to confuse the French. Those men had caught up with them the day before and now the camp was the usual sprawl of tents, cooking fires, hastily erected washing lines, and people everywhere. It covered several acres and the rest of the army's arrival had swollen the already huge conglomeration of soldiers, wives, mistresses and children. Not to mention the sutlers, blacksmiths, whores and whoremasters, herdsmen and tradesmen – the usual trail of hangers-on that an army on the march produced. Marching to Badajoz was a slow business.

Richard Camberwell walked thoughtfully back to the tent he shared with his fellow captain, James Shaw. He found the officer lying on his cot, smoking a cigar, trying to make smoke rings. Camberwell sat wearily on his own narrow bed.

"Any luck with the Frenchie?" he asked.

"He's part of half a battalion on its way to Badajoz," said Shaw. The captain was a tall, fair-haired, handsome man, not much given to hard work but content to do what was needed and laze around the rest of the time. He was, however, charming and a great hit with the ladies. Although Camberwell sometimes found his indolence a little frustrating, they had been together for several months now. Richard Camberwell had the grace to know that not many people would put up with his own sharp temper and Shaw was so easy going it was hard for Camberwell to imagine sharing a billet with any other officer.

"The frog wasn't very forthcoming. All that I managed to get out of him was that the garrison at Badajoz had wind of our coming and sent for reinforcements," Shaw said now. He sucked again on the cigar and blew out gently, the smoke forming a perfect ring. "Damn! I'm good," he said, which made Camberwell smile. Shaw looked more serious when he carried on. "The son-of-a-bitch actually laughed when I said they were wasting their time. That we'll over-run the bastards anyway, however many of them there are. Says Badajoz is impregnable. You ever seen it, Richard? Is it impregnable?"

Camberwell picked up a bottle from beside his cot and poured a small glass full of brandy, the last of the supply he had gleaned from the beaten French at Cuidad Roderigo. He drained it in one gulp. "I've never seen it," he answered. "But I've heard tales. Badajoz is supposed to be huge, much bigger than Ciudad Rodrigo, and a strange shape."

"What do you mean?"

"There are star shaped crenellations at each corner, and every one of those tagged on pieces is a fort in itself, then at one end of the town is a castle. There are also outlying forts as well. From what I hear it's going to be a tough nut to crack."

Shaw said nothing but continued to blow smoke into the small tent. Richard Camberwell poured another glass of brandy and thought back to his life before Spain. Then his main worries were which of his horses to take out for a gallop in the morning. As the heir to a large estate in the south of England he had responsibilities, but his mother was active and held the purse strings with a strong hand. His had been an easy life until he had joined the army as a lieutenant two years before. There had always been that restlessness though, that feeling, even as a boy, that the placid country life was not for him. And as soon as he had been sent to the Peninsula he had felt the restrictions of lord of the manor fall away and he enjoyed the spice and danger that the army added to his life. Yes, there were times when boredom set in, and he was often cold, wet, and hungry, but on the whole he thought he had been born to army life and wondered if he would ever be able to settle back to being a civilian again one day.

This thought took his mind to his servant, Will Tucker. Will had also taken to the army like the proverbial duck to water. He smiled, thinking of the thief Will had been. The previous year, when Camberwell had been back in England recuperating from a serious wound, Will had stolen his purse and ten guineas, then redeemed himself by saving his life. Camberwell had taken him on as a stable hand to pay back his debt in kind but then the army had intervened, as had his niece, Megan, who had run off with Will to join the army. Now Will and Megan were part of this mix of humanity that had been sent to the Iberian Peninsula to beat back the French, as was Sarah Harvey, another stowaway on the ship that had brought them here, and who was now Camberwell's lover. So much had changed in all their lives since their arrival in Portugal last October and he wondered what lay ahead at Badajoz.

His description of the fortified town that lay south of the mountains had been a true one. It was a difficult, heavily guarded place that the French thought impregnable but Richard Camberwell knew the reason why Wellington wanted to besiege it. The taking of Cuidad Roderigo had been necessary to open up the northern part of Spain as it guarded the only road good enough to take the British heavy artillery. Badajoz guarded the only road further south that was needed for the same thing. They had to take it. If they didn't, there was no point in continuing the war. It would become a mess of small, inconclusive battles to hold the mountainous regions, and would go no further. Spain was a big country with important towns and ports and the British government was determined that Napoleon Bonaparte would not be allowed to carry out his plan of complete European domination.

Camberwell's thoughts were interrupted by the sudden, noisy arrival of his niece, Megan, who pushed aside the tent flap without so much as a request to enter and stood with her hands on her hips, frowning angrily.

"Uncle, please tell Will that he has to leave that damn dog alone and brush your dress jacket for the parade tomorrow!" she said angrily. "He says I must do it! I've got enough of my own things to see to. And he hasn't left that bloody dog alone since it came here!"

Richard Camberwell surveyed his sixteen-year-old niece and tried in vain to hide a smile. Megan Camberwell was as short-tempered as he was himself and did not make any attempt to hide her annoyance when things displeased her. Now her green eyes were flashing as she glared at him.

Forcing back the smile, he put on a suitably serious face but not to help her with her request. "Megan, how many times have I told you not to come in here without giving us some notice of your intention?" he said. "What if Captain Shaw or I had been changing our clothes, or one of us had been entertaining a lady?"

"Stuff and nonsense!" said Megan airily. "You have nothing to change for this evening and Sarah's busy helping at Lily Mark's birthing. As for you, Captain," she turned to James Shaw who was watching her with some amusement, "I know for a fact that you aren't seeing anyone at the moment so it's unlikely I'd be interrupting anything." She glared at her uncle again. "Now what are you going to do about Will? He's your servant. Order him to brush your uniform!"

"I'll ask Dodge to do it," said Camberwell. "Will must be cooking now, isn't he?"

"Well … yes. In between looking after that flea-bag." Megan suddenly smiled, lighting up her face and showing something of its true beauty, glad that she didn't have to see to her uncle's jacket. "Thank you. I'll tell Dodge to do it then, shall I?"

"Yes, you can do that if he's finished mending Captain Shaw's spare trousers. And tell Will to come and see me when he can get away from the cooking fire for five minutes."

"If I can get him away from that blasted dog, you mean!" Megan said wryly as she went out.

"Stop swearing!" Richard Camberwell shouted after her. He turned at the sound of Shaw's laughter. "And you can stop that," he said, half amused himself. "You don't help matters when you encourage her."

"Who me?" said James Shaw with pretended innocence. "What did I do?"

"It's what you don't do," grumbled Camberwell. "You treat her like she's your sister instead of a Lady. She's forgetting her up-bringing and the good manners her grand-mother instilled in her."

James Shaw doubted very much whether Lady Megan Camberwell had ever had good manners or the genteel disposition required of female English aristocracy, but he didn't say this to his friend. He knew that although Richard Camberwell had been forced into allowing her to come to Spain in the first place, he was not happy about her being there. He was glad that she had friends and that they had helped her to come to terms with her lot as much as she was able, but it irked him that some of the camp followers' language and behaviour had rubbed off on her as well.

Richard Camberwell's grumbling was not improved when a black nose poked its way into the tent's opening and Will could be heard outside admonishing the dog it belonged to.

"Get out'v it, Scrapper! The Cap'n'll treat yer worse'n the Frenchies did if yer go in there!"

This was followed by a growl and a scuffle while the tent's canvas caved in to the rhythmic beating of the dog's tail, then Will's face appeared. "Yer wanted ter see me, sir?" he asked.

"Yes, but keep that hairy beast out of here," said Camberwell, sourly, sitting on the only chair that stood beside the small table. He scowled at Will as the boy entered the tent. "What have you done with it?"

"Tied 'im ter the tent pole, Captain," Will answered. The tail was still buffeting the side of the tent.

"Make it lie down," said Camberwell. "It'll have the bloody tent over at this rate."

"I'll try, sir," said Will. "But 'e ain't much of a one fer takin' orders as yet." Will went outside and spoke sharply to the animal who, pleased to see his new master, jumped up against the tent on his two good back legs, causing both officers to wonder if Camberwell's prophecy might not come true. Eventually Will managed to get the dog settled down and he came back inside.

"What did yer want me for, sir?" he asked. "Only the stew's boilin' an' I don't want ter burn it."

"All right, all right! I'll only keep you a minute." Will listened impassively. He was well used to Richard Camberwell's irritability and ignored most of his petulant anger. "I want you to take some food to the French prisoner later and see what you can find out. The captain here's had a word with him, but I've a feelin' he might tell you things he won't tell James. We'd like to know when the French are planning to move on. Maybe if they're going to stay where they are for a day or two, we'll have time to give them a little reminder that they're not the only ones in Spain who have an interest in Badajoz. Be nice to the fellow, Will. Pretend to be his friend."

"Aye, sir." Will pushed back the lock of dirty blond hair that continually fell into his eyes. "Is that all, sir?"

"Yes. No. Megan says you're spending far too much time with that animal."

Will grinned, not surprised that she had already complained. "She would, sir. I'll do yer jacket after supper."

"Don't bother. I've already got Dodge on the job. But if that beast interferes with your work, lad, it'll have to go. Understand?"

"O' course, sir. Me an' Scrapper'll do all right, never yer worry. And I'll get back ter yer when I've seen the Frenchie, sir. Supper'll be less 'n 'alf an hour – if it ain't burned by now!" he added cheekily.

"Go and see to it, you rogue," said Camberwell in mock anger. "And make sure I get a good helping. All that business today's made me extra hungry."

"Yes, sir,' said Will, still smiling, and he went out of the tent to be greeted boisterously by Scrapper whose tail proceeded to beat the tent wall again.

"Will!" shouted Camberwell.

"Yes, sir! Goin', sir!" Will shouted back

"I sometimes wonder why I keep that lad on," Richard Camberwell muttered as he searched for his pen amongst the papers on the table, in preparation for writing up his report of the earlier skirmish. Once found, he settled down to write. "What sort of a name is Scrapper anyway?"

Lying on his cot with his hands clasped behind his head, James Shaw laughed but did not reply. He let his thoughts wander. He knew exactly why his fellow officer kept Will around. Apart from the fact that the lad had saved Megan's life and helped bring a traitor to justice just a few weeks ago, he was a good cook and a wonder with the horses. He also knew how to deal with his master's moods – and not many knew how to do that. There was, too, the budding relationship between Will and Megan – one that had started off badly and would not have even been considered some months ago. But things had changed. Their lives had changed. And now it was well known in the battalion that Will and Megan were more than good friends, though Shaw was almost certain that there had been nothing physical between the two as yet. Despite Will treating her as any other girl, Shaw suspected that the lad still had respect for her breeding and doubted he would do anything of a sexual nature without the benefit of marriage, and that would be a long time coming. Richard Camberwell knew of their relationship but would not condone anything unorthodox.

James Shaw wondered how Will was coping with that side of things. According to the female camp followers, some of whom Shaw knew intimately, Will was considered a catch, having good looks and a pleasant personality. Then there was Juanita, the whore back in the hillside village where they had spent the winter months. It still hurt Shaw to think of her because she had become his lover before succumbing to Amos Wilkins's knife. He had loved her, but she had also had a thing for Will, despite him being much younger. Yes. Will was very attractive to the female sex and James Shaw couldn't see him being too happy about having to wait for marriage to entertain Megan in that fashion.

His thoughts were broken by Will's shout that food was ready. With Richard Camberwell exclaiming that it was about time too, Shaw followed his friend from the tent.

Chapter 2

After supper, Will filled a bowl with the watery stew and took it to the French prisoner who was sitting under guard and tethered to a tree. The bored soldier guarding him took the opportunity of Will's presence to take himself off for his own supper. The Frenchman, rather pale and dishevelled, smiled his thanks and ate with only one hand, the other arm being in a sling. Will sat and watched him as he made short work of the stew. The Frenchman was young, probably only in his early twenties, with a fresh face and brown hair. Will liked the look of him. Despite having done his fair share of killing the young fellow's countrymen in the past few months, he was of the opinion that the French were only doing a job, as he was, and that they had the same hopes, fears and needs as he did. He sat down on the grass in front of the prisoner.

"What's yer name, then?" he asked. His knowledge of French was almost non-existent but he knew that a lot of the French had a smattering of English.

"Alain," said the man through a mouthful of tough beef. "Alain de Ferrier."

"I'm Will Tucker," said Will. "Bin in the army long, 'ave yer?"

The young man shook his head. "*Non. Quatre* … er …" He held up four fingers. Will assumed that meant four months. The Frenchman suddenly spat an angry mouthful of French, obviously annoyed that he had been captured so soon.

Will let the man eat until the bowl was empty, then pointed to the man's arm. "'Ow is it?"

"It is … 'ow you say? Sore?" said the man leaning back against the tree.

Will nodded. "Can I get yer anythin'?"

"*Oui*. A knife to cut zis rope," said de Ferrier sarcastically.

Will laughed. "Not a chance," he said. "But I can get someone ter look at yer arm if yer like."

"*Non*. It 'as already been. It is a flesh wound. I will live," said de Ferrier gloomily. "It is better I should die," he said. "Ze shame …"

"There's no shame in bein' taken prisoner unless it were yer own fault," said Will philosophically, remembering his own brief incarceration by the

British authorities at Ciudad Rodrigo which had certainly been due to bad judgement on his part. He was distracted for a moment by Scrapper who bounded up to him in a sort of lop-sided run and licked his face enthusiastically. Alain de Ferrier stared in amazement. "Zat is ze dog Jean shot!" he exclaimed. "'E is yours?"

"'E is now," said Will. "Gerroff yer daft bugger!" The dog sat down and, with a final lick at Will's ear, proceeded to have a good scratch at a stray flea.

There was silence while the prisoner watched Will stroking and talking to the dog, then he said, "What will 'appen to me?"

Will shrugged. "Yer not an officer."

"*Non*," de Ferrier agreed.

"Then yer'll probably be sent ter Lisbon or Madrid and put in jail 'til the end o' the war."

There were more angry words as de Ferrier struggled with this information. Will felt a pang of sympathy for the young man. He knew how much he would hate to be imprisoned. When he had been incarcerated for a while back in Ciudad Rodrigo he had escaped at the first opportunity.

He thought he'd better try and find out the information Captain Camberwell had asked for. "What're yer friends doin' 'ere?" he asked.

De Ferrier gave him a sharp look and then realised he had already imparted this information to the officer who had interrogated him a short while before. "We go to Badajoz," he said. "To 'elp fight against you."

"Goin' soon, are yer?" asked Will innocently.

"We rest for three days. We 'ave to rest ze 'orses but my Colonel may go sooner now. 'E will know you are 'ere."

Will knew this was so. The French would want to reach Badajoz before the British. "'Ow long yer bin 'ere, then?" he asked.

"We stop yesterday. Ze 'orses, zey 'ave worked 'ard. We did not rest for two days …" De Ferrier suddenly realised he might be giving away too much information and stopped speaking. Will hardly noticed. He was thinking. It would seem that if Wellington wanted to discourage this small part of the French army from further participation he would have to do it soon.

De Ferrier picked up a cup of water that Will had brought, and drained it. "*Merci*," he said. "I will rest now." He leaned back against the tree and closed his eyes. Realising he would learn nothing more, Will picked up the cup and empty bowl, called Scrapper who was chewing on an old bone he had found nearby, then walked back to Captain Camberwell's tent.

Richard Camberwell was pleased with the news that Will imparted. He went immediately to tell Wellington who called for his senior officers. They talked well into the night, planning an early march towards the French.

"This is just what we need," said Lieutenant-Colonel Davenport, the Light Division's commanding officer, eagerly to Richard Camberwell much later in the former's tent. He had called for his captains despite the late hour, to inform them of the strategy meeting's outcome. "A battle now will demoralise the French," he continued enthusiastically. "Let them know we mean business, eh? Wellington's given permission for my battalion to do the honours. Four companies should do it." He winced, held his stomach, and let out an enormous belch, then turned an anguished face to his servant. "Good God, man! What the devil did you put in that beef tonight? Bullets? My stomach feels like a lump of lead!"

The poor servant, a frequent butt for Davenport's ill-humour, blushed and stuttered and said he would find some physic with which to ease his master's chronic indigestion, then gratefully escaped the tent. Richard Camberwell and the other officers waited patiently for Davenport to continue.

"We leave at four." Davenport turned to Camberwell. "Your Company will lead, Richard, as you know where the bastards are …"

"Sir," Camberwell interrupted. "We only saw smoke. I don't know exactly where they are."

"Don't quibble, man. You know the general direction. That's good enough. If they're still there, we'll find 'em. Make sure your men have ammunition, water, and enough rations to see the day out. The prisoner says they should be there for another day, but we may have scared them into leaving early. If they've gone, we may have to follow them."

"Yes, sir." There was general agreement from the officers who were then dismissed. Richard Camberwell walked back to his tent thoughtfully. He knew that an attack from the rear was something Marshall Marmont, the commander of Napoleon's army in the north, would not suspect, would not even know about, as he was impotently miles away, cut off by the now Spanish-held Ciudad Rodrigo. If they could prevent, or even delay, French troops from reaching Badajoz, it would help when it came to taking the fortress itself. He had bad feelings about Badajoz. The British were on a high at the moment. The taking of Ciudad Rodrigo had been hard, yet the army had been victorious, and the few weeks after, spent resting and attending to the wounded, had been filled with good food, wine, and women from the beleaguered town. The men were happy despite the hard slog and bad weather of the march, but Richard Camberwell had a horrible feeling they would not be happy for much longer. Badajoz was a different kettle of fish altogether, or so he had heard, and the taking of Ciudad Rodrigo would be child's play in comparison.

Pushing through the canvas flap he found the tent empty which suited his mood. Shaw was probably with one of the camp's whores. He took off his jacket and threw it onto the chair, loosened his shirt and hunted around James Shaw's cot for another bottle of wine. Finding one, he pulled the cork and tipped it up, drinking a good draught before crashing onto his cot so hard that it creaked ominously. Drinking and thinking, he did not sleep. He could not rid himself of a sense of unease that stayed with him into the pre-dawn hours of the morning when he sat on Hades's back, nursing a thumping head and a rolling stomach, waiting for Lieutenant-Colonel Davenport to order the men to move out.

His hangover and lack of sleep did nothing for his temper and Will bore the brunt of it. "You can't take that damn mutt with you, Will! Tie it to a tree or something until we get back!" he said angrily. Scrapper was limping around Hades's hooves, barking madly, infected by the excitement and activity. "Take it away, damn you!"

"Aye, sir," said Will, lining up with the rest of the Company. He had had no intention of taking Scrapper into a battle anyway, but the animal now looked upon him as a constant companion and followed him everywhere. With difficulty he dragged the dog away and tied a rope around his neck. "Come on, yer daft 'aporth!" he said. "Molly'll look after yer 'til I get back." He dragged the unwilling animal to a patched tent and tied him, whining, to a nearby tree. A girl was standing nearby, heavily entwined with a young soldier, Will's friend, Bob Tomkins. "Look after 'im, Molly," said Will, giving Scrapper a last hug.

"I'll do me best, Will," said the girl loudly. "An' you be careful, an' all."

"Yes, you do that, Will," said a softer voice and Will turned round to see Megan in a nightgown with her cloak over the top. Her hair was tousled from sleep but her face was beautiful, and Will's heart did a flip at the sight of her. He took her in his arms. "I will," he said, quietly, and kissed her gently on the lips. "Take more'n a bunch of Frenchmen ter put me away."

Megan Camberwell looked up into the thin, mischievous face that was split by a huge grin, and wondered at herself. Will Tucker was a rogue, a street urchin who had picked pockets to survive the mean streets of London Town. Way down at the bottom of her social ladder. And he loved being a soldier. Mad in her opinion, yet she loved him with all her heart. There was a dead weight in her stomach at the thought of him going off to fight, of the dangers he would have to face. But, like all the women who followed the army, she had to pretend that there was nothing in it, that it was just another job, and bravely face the fact that she might never see him again. Just the thought brought tears to her eyes, but then she heard Molly say to her beau, Bob Tomkins, "You just give them French bastards a tickle up the back-side, Bob," and it made her laugh so that she could say her goodbyes to Will without a tear being shed. She knew that the moment the men had gone she would have to spend hours rolling bandages, most of them taken from men who had already worn them and died in them. She had helped to scrub the blood away, but they were still stained, and she knew from bitter experience that they would be bloody again before the day was out. She just hoped that Will wouldn't be needing one of them.

*

Will watched the feeble dawn rise above the hills. It was cloudy and cold but at least marching warmed one up. The men were quiet for the most part and the sound of tramping feet and horses' hooves, coughs and sniffs, and the creak of saddle leather was all that could be heard as the column moved in the direction Camberwell's small patrol had taken the day before. He wondered if the French would know they were coming. They weren't stupid. They would have their own Exploring Officers out, wouldn't they? How far were they from Badajoz? He didn't know. Would they surprise the French? It seemed a bit of a hit-or-miss situation to him.

"How far now, you bastard?" A sergeant's voice rang out loudly and Will watched him cuff the ear of the young Frenchman, de Ferrier, who was walking just ahead of him, his hands tied behind his back. Despite Lieutenant-Colonel Davenport's optimistic opinion that they would easily find the French, it had been decided that the prisoner should be taken along to avoid wasting time and he was now giving them directions. Will wondered if he had thought to lead them on a false trail, but decided that he would have been stupid to do so. Richard Camberwell knew the general direction and would know immediately if they were being misled.

They had passed the spot where the small patrol had encountered the French and the dog. "About an hour, maybe more," muttered de Ferrier who was a very unwilling participant and had earned himself several clubs from the sergeant's fist for not being specific enough in his information. Now he received another clout on the head.

"Which way?" shouted the sergeant. They had come to a sloping hillside. One goat path led up, another around. The young man winced and pointed around. The sergeant shouted to Camberwell in front and the column turned to the right, skirting the hill.

After another fifty minutes marching they saw a haze of smoke from the top of a gentle rise and heard distant shouting. Richard Camberwell sent Hades back down the slope and gave orders that the men rest for a while.

"Will, I want you to go and scout their camp," he said. "I need to know the layout so that I can plan the attack."

"Yes, sir." Will nodded. Excitement bubbled up in him. His was an important job. The outcome of the mission might depend on him.

"You'd best borrow a horse," said Camberwell and Will's heart sank. He loved looking after horses but riding them was a different matter. He was better at it than he used to be, but still not proficient, especially on the temperamental beasts the officers rode. Lightfoot, Megan's first pony who was anything but light on his feet, was all he could ride well, but he was back at the British camp.

"Ride Hades," said Camberwell and handed him the reins. Relieved, Will scrambled onto the horse's back. At least he knew Hades, having groomed and fed him for the last six months. Hades whickered and stepped sideways but Will leaned over and patted his neck, speaking soothing words. Hades stood still again, recognizing his voice. Will kicked back his heels and Hades trotted off in the direction of the smoke.

It took Will less than three minutes to reach a vantage point from where he could look down on the French camp and what he saw made him gasp. The French were preparing to move out. They had some of their guns limbered up ready to go, a few men were kicking out smoking camp fires, and a lot of the troops were filing into marching order already. There were no sentries. Quickly Will ran back down the slope to where Hades waited patiently for him, lifted his foot for the stirrup, missed it and fell, got to his feet and tried again. This time he made it and pulled himself into the saddle then raced back towards the British, clinging onto the reins and the horse's mane for dear life.

Hades slithered to a halt, raising a cloud of dust and Will slid from the saddle, nearly falling again in his haste and anxiety. "They're leaving, sir!" he said to Camberwell who was taking the opportunity to smoke a cigar. "They're getting ready to march!"

"Damn!" Camberwell ground the cigar out under his foot. If they weren't quick they might as well go back to camp. Chasing the French on the move would be a waste of time and effort. "How many?" he asked.

"'Alf a battalion, I'd say," Will answered.

Five Companies. Probably less than four hundred men. Most of the French and British battalions were well under full strength now the war was getting old, depleted by battle and sickness. Yet these French reinforcements still outnumbered his four Companies. Quickly, he rapped out orders and the resting men picked up their muskets and ran into ranks. "Do they have guns?" he asked Will.

"Yes, sir. Six pounders and 'owitzers."

"Damn!" If the French turned the guns on the British they stood no chance. The only saving grace was that if the guns were ready for travelling, it would take some time to prepare them for attack.

Every minute counted and the British knew it. They jogged along until they came to the point where Will had stopped. They could hear voices now as well as the jingle of harness and the rumble of wheels. Richard Camberwell had a hurried conversation with the other officers which ended with two companies going right and left while Camberwell led his own and another up the sloping ground that was feathered with tufts of hardy grass between scattered small trees and rocks. Near the top of the hill they fell into line on the grass but just out of sight of the French.

Camberwell's men lay on their stomachs with their weapons beside them and surveyed the scene below. It appeared to be ordered chaos. Will was relieved to see that the French had been held up. A wheel had fallen off a limber and another gun was stuck in the ruts of the muddy track. Men were trying to urge the horses pulling the impacted artillery while others were searching baggage for hammers and nails with which to fix the wheel. Many of the soldiers Will had seen ready to march were now resting beside the track, not seeming to be in any hurry to move on.

The French had camped on a flat piece of ground beside the track that Will presumed led to Badajoz. The ridge the British were on sloped down on one side until it reached the ground in a tumble of large rocks. A few small trees and the rocks were the only shelter.

"Will, take George, Bob, and Nat down the slope to those rocks." Richard Camberwell spoke quietly and pointed to the rocks near the bottom of the slope. "Take out the men around those stuck guns." Will nodded and went to fetch the others. The four of them crept down the slope, taking cover behind stunted trees until they reached the rocks. Each man chose a target and suddenly the shouts and disturbance around the French artillery was interrupted by the cracks of rifles that, at this range, could not miss. There were cries of surprise and pain as men fell while some of the soldiers hurried for cover, hastily trying to load muskets and return the fire at the tell-tale puffs of smoke that wafted up in the air from the rocks at the bottom of the slope.

Such was their distraction, none of the French noticed that the ridge was suddenly full of the enemy until Camberwell's orders rang out and the air was filled with the deadly whine of rifle and musket balls.

The chaos below quickly worsened. Amidst a string of shouted orders and screams from the wounded, the French tried to rally but the damage had already been done. The British companies that had gone around the ridge formed a pincer movement and stood calmly in line firing volleys some fifty yards either side of the French – a distance that compensated for the musket's notorious inaccuracy. Will was disinclined to shoot as the enemy were frantically trying to find cover and mostly ignoring orders from their officers to return fire. He felt rather sorry for them, but then the cry came, "'Ware cavalry! Form square!" A group of forty or so horsemen, already mounted and some distance away from their colleagues' confusion, had seen the danger and come to the rescue of their infantry. Showing no perceptible hurry, the red-coated company in danger on the flat ground nearest to the approaching cavalry shuffled itself into a tight square. There was the scrape of metal against metal and the front row on all sides knelt down, their bayonets forming a razor sharp fence around the men – a fence that no horse would attempt to cross. Frustrated, the cavalry milled impotently around it while the second row of British soldiers fired at them from all four sides of the square, eventually forcing the mounted horsemen to retire to a safe distance.

The British were fewer in number but the element of surprise had given them the advantage. Through the swirling smoke Will saw a Colonel attempting to form the French soldiers into a column, their usual method of attack, but it was difficult. An artillery captain was shouting at men to turn the guns so that they could rake the square with gun-fire but the lines of British were too close and the gun crews were more concerned with taking cover. One enterprising French sergeant managed to turn a six-pounder around and shouted at his team to load it up. The British square was a tempting target with the men packed so closely together. Only a few of the French were returning the British fire. The attack from three sides meant that the dead and wounded were falling and getting in the way, and the milling cavalry horses were actually doing more harm than good, but the artillery meant a real threat.

"Get that artillery!" shouted Camberwell who, from the top of the ridge, immediately saw the danger. Will clambered back up the hillside a little, the better to see what was going on. Others followed, and the soldiers of the Light Company, men with rifles that had the range and accuracy, aimed at the frantic gunners. Shots rang out and all but two of the gunners fell. Will quickly felt for another cartridge. The smoke was now so heavy he wasn't sure he had shot anyone but he had aimed in the right direction. The rifle barrel was hot and his cheek was already black with powder burns. He bit off the end of the paper cartridge and performed the loading movements that had now become second nature. He wondered what was going on beyond the rocks. There were screams and shouts, the whine of bullets, but it was becoming increasingly difficult to see anything. Then the small wind blew a skein of smoke away so that, for a moment, he could make out the French, and what he saw made his heart leap. "They're goin', sir!" he shouted.

"What?" Camberwell, now running down the slope towards him, could hardly hear for the noise.

"The Frenchies! They're runnin' away!" shouted Will, pointing down the track.

The French had indeed stopped firing and the smoke was beginning to thin. Through gaps in the grey mist they could see that the cavalry was already galloping away and that the French were broken. Officers were still trying to force their men into some sort of defence but they were fighting a losing battle. These were not battle-hardened warriors and the surprise attack had scared them. Men were running after the guns that were being pulled down the muddy track by horses also eager to get away from the noise and confusion. Wounded colleagues were helped but the dead were left in the dirt. The limber that was stuck in the mud and the other with the broken wheel, were forgotten in the rush to get away, the guns they held left behind for the British. A French Colonel stood up in his stirrups and shook his fist at the British on the hill, his angry shouts taken away by the wind. Will lifted his rifle but Camberwell pushed the barrel down. "Leave it, Will," he said quietly. "They've had enough. Cease fire!" he shouted to the few men still sending musket balls after the retreating enemy and he heard his orders repeated by the officers of the other two companies. Soon all that could be heard was a faint thud of hooves and tramping feet as the French hurried towards the safety of Badajoz.

The British boys cheered. Those on the ridge scampered down its slope, eager to pilfer what they could from the dead bodies. Richard Camberwell shouted to Sergeant Readman. "Bring me a butcher's bill, Sergeant, as soon as you can!"

"Yes, sir," came the reply and Readman went to count the British dead and wounded.

"Looks like they suffered a lot more than us," said Camberwell to Will.

"Yes, sir," said Will. He could see very few red-coated figures lying on the ground but a lot of blue ones. "Gave them a taste of what's to come," Camberwell continued. "I'm amazed they had no sentries or patrols out. They must have known we were in the area. Surely someone must have missed those men we killed yesterday."

Will also thought it strange that they had not come across any more French patrols. He shrugged. "Maybe their cavalry was scoutin', sir. P'raps that was why they were leavin'. Remember the prisoner back at camp said 'e thought they might leave early after what 'appened yesterday."

Camberwell nodded. "Well, there's some that won't be fighting us, and hopefully that's the last we see of the rest before we reach Badajoz," he said, then turned his attention to Sergeant Readman who was puffing up the slope towards them. "Butcher's bill, sir," he panted. Readman was a heavily built, stocky man who liked his ale and was not built for climbing hills. "None dead, five wounded – two serious, sir," he said.

"Could be worse," said Camberwell. "Get them back to camp as soon as you can, Readman. Make stretchers with muskets and jackets for the wounded if they can't walk." He turned towards Captain Shaw who was at the other end of the slope. "Captain! Get the men into ranks. They can come back and bury their dead if they want to. Let's get back to camp."

The march back to the British camp was a jubilant one. The men reached it full of themselves and their victory, but their mood was soon dampened because no one at camp seemed eager to hear their good news.

"What's up?" Will had been met by a joyous Scrapper who seemed the only being pleased to see him. Molly was looking downcast, not even relieved to see that Bob had returned unharmed. "What is it, Molly? What's 'appened?"

Molly's tear-filled eyes stared at Will. "While you were gone some girls went down to the stream to bathe and do their laundry. They went to that place over there, be'ind the bushes, to be more private, like." She pointed to a clump of bushes some two hundred yards away where the small stream ran in twists and turns and hid itself from the camp. "A French patrol sneaked up on 'em. First anyone 'ere knew, was when we 'eard the screams. By the time anyone got there the French were riding away with 'em. Only dirty washing and some o' their clothes left on the ground." Tears ran down her cheeks as she looked at Will. "Megan was there, Will. She was with 'em. The French have got 'er, Will. Megan's gone!"

Chapter 3

For a moment, Will gaped at Molly, hardly able to take in her dreadful news. He felt numb, unable to move, then realisation set in and he started to run towards the track that led to Badajoz, rescuing Megan the only thought in his head.

Suddenly a strong hand grabbed him by the arm and he was pulled around to face Sergeant Readman. "'Old up there, lad," said the sergeant quietly. "I 'ear they've already sent out a search party."

Will stared at the bluff sergeant and could not help the tears that pricked his eyes. Angrily he cuffed them away. "Why wasn't there a guard with 'em?" he shouted. "'Ow could Frenchies get that close ter the camp without anyone seein'?"

The sergeant sighed and shrugged. "Mebbe the girls wanted privacy, lad," he said. "An' no one was expectin' any Frenchies. We were fightin' the only ones in the area, weren't we?"

"Like 'ell!" shouted Will. "There still should've bin sentries watchin'."

Sergeant Readman privately agreed but his main task now was to stop Will going off after the enemy, not to argue the point. "Come on, lad. Talk to the captain. He's as upset about it as you are. Megan's 'is niece, you know."

Will realised the sergeant was right. Richard Camberwell must be worried and talking to him would be a good idea, so he went to the captain's tent where Richard Camberwell was ranting at two unfortunate soldiers who had apparently been told to stand guard while the girls bathed.

"It were Lady Camberwell, sir," mumbled one of them in their defence.

"What's that? Speak up, man! I can't hear you!" shouted Camberwell, pacing the short distance between his cot and the tent flap, then back again.

"It were Lady Camberwell," said the man again, a little louder. "She told us to go away. Was worried we'd take a peek, sir. Though God knows we'd never," he added hurriedly, his face turning red with embarrassment. "Yer knows that, sir."

"Since when is Lady Camberwell your officer, man?" Camberwell roared, stopping his pacing and ending up so close to the soldier that the young man took a step backwards and bumped into his colleague who was staring at the ground, the same shame mirrored on his face.

The soldier who had spoken gathered his startled wits and seemed to be searching for some words that would not anger the irate officer further. "Lady Megan ... she ... er ... she can be a bit forceful at times, sir," he managed. "Said she'd tell Lieutenant-Colonel Davenport if we didn't go back to camp. Threatened us with a floggin' sir, she did. So we went, sir. Didn't think there'd be any more Frenchies about, sir."

Richard Camberwell made a loud noise of disgust. It was just the sort of thing Megan would do. Even now, there were still times when she remembered she was a Lady and would frighten the rank and file with her scathing tongue. Good God! What was he to do? He ran fingers through his hair in frustration.

"Go!" he said to the two men. "Davenport will hear about this and if he has you flogged, it's no more than you deserve!" The two men crept out and Richard Camberwell noticed Will for the first time.

"What are we goin' ter do, sir?" asked Will, his face as dirty white as the tent canvas.

Camberwell did not reply but sat down in his chair and stared at him for some seconds with much the same expression of despair before saying, "By all accounts there were only three or four of the enemy but they had no problem in subduing the three girls." He was quiet for a moment and stared down at the table next to the chair. When he looked up at Will again, his eyes were haunted. "Sarah was one, Will. Both gone. Megan and Sarah."

Will gasped. It was even worse than he thought. Sarah, the girl Richard Camberwell loved. Sarah, who had followed the captain to war and stowed away on the same ship as he and Megan. The quiet, tender-hearted girl who was a good nurse and Megan's best friend. It was probably she who had suggested the bathe as she was always conscious of the poor hygienic conditions they lived in, but why, oh why, had Megan sent the guards away?

"What can we do?" he asked again.

"Wait and see if the patrol finds them, I suppose," was the reply.

"And if they don't?" Will was itching to do something, anything, and sitting waiting was the worst thing he could be doing at the moment.

Camberwell's sad eyes stared into his. "Davenport says once they find out Megan's aristocracy they'll take them to Badajoz and ask for a ransom. Well, her anyway. What they'll do with Sarah and Amy Rogers I can only guess at."

Will could guess too, and his thoughts were not very pleasant. Sarah was pretty in an elfin sort of way, and Amy Rogers, the young wife of a soldier in B Company, was not ugly. They would be ripe for the plucking.

"If the search party doesn't find 'em, I'm goin' ter," he said defiantly.

Richard Camberwell gave him a sad half smile. "I think we're only a day or so's march from Badajoz, Will. They've got a good head start. If our lads don't catch up with them, they'll be stashed away behind the walls before we get there."

"Ain't yer goin' ter do anythin'?" Will stared at his master in disbelief.

"Yes, Will." Camberwell's voice was stronger. "It's killing me to do it, but I'm going to wait for the search party to come back. We're moving out in the morning. In the meantime there are a hundred things to do …"

"Captain Shaw can see ter those," Will interrupted strongly. "If the patrol comes back empty-'anded, what then?"

"Then I'll ask permission to go ahead of the column," Camberwell promised. "And we'll find them, Will. We'll find them."

That afternoon everything seemed to go awry in the British camp. It started to rain and the ground that had been drying out in the wind soon became a quagmire again. Cooking fires spluttered out and men sat miserably in tents if they had them, otherwise sheltered as best they could under the sparse trees. The commissary's reserves of flour got wet and Lieutenant-Colonel Davenport's servant dropped and broke a case of his favourite wine. Then disaster struck Richard Camberwell. He was helping to move Hades and some of the other officers' horses onto drier ground when he stumbled over a slippery tree root. The horse nearest to him, startled by the cry and sudden movement as Camberwell fell, lashed out with his hoof and kicked him hard on the ankle. Camberwell knew immediately the injury was serious. Will, who had been on the other side of the horses, saw his master fall and ran to his aid.

Camberwell lay on the ground, clutching his ankle, his face paper white. "It's broken, Will," he ground out through clenched teeth. "Best get Barker."

John Barker was the battalion surgeon. He soon confirmed what Richard Camberwell already knew. "Take that boot off before the swelling gets too much, lad," he said to Will, kneeling down beside the stricken man while the rain poured down on all of them "Easy now. That's it." Camberwell winced as Will removed his boot. Barker, not the most tender of men, roughly felt the injured ankle and Will saw Camberwell grit his teeth. "Aye, it's broken, sir. Nought to do but splint it and bandage it up. You won't be doin' much runnin' for a while," the surgeon said cheerfully. Richard Camberwell muttered swear words and slammed his fist onto the wet grass.

Will was sent to look for suitable sticks to use as splints and as he did so he wondered about the captain's plans for trying to find Megan and the others. The patrol had still not returned and he reckoned they had been gone over five hours. They had left barely minutes after the girls had been taken. Surely they would have seen some sign of them by now. It was very worrying. He set his mind to looking for stout sticks and went back to help the surgeon but he couldn't help thinking of Megan and hoped she was all right.

*

Megan Camberwell was angry. She had never been so cross, and most of her anger was directed at herself. It had been an act of sheer stupidity to send the sentries away. How many times had her uncle told her never to stray far from the camp alone? She had thought that having the other two girls with her was security enough, and they had so little privacy. This was all her fault. She glanced across at the two girls who, like her, were sitting on horses behind the Frenchmen who had taken them. Sarah was pale and looked frightened. Amy Rogers was crying. The Frenchmen had galloped away with their prizes but had now slowed their horses down to a canter. They were talking loudly, grinning and looking extremely happy, as no doubt they were. Especially since they had known the British would chase them, had waited at a bend in the track and shot at the soldiers, killing three and wounding two. Megan had been afraid that Will or her uncle were with the search party but had realised even as the poor men were being shot at, that Will and Camberwell would not have been back from their own battle in time to follow them. It was possible that they did not yet know about their abduction.

She looked down at her filthy dress. She was lucky to have it on. If she hadn't bathed quickly and come out of the cold water when she had, she would still only have her underclothes on like Sarah and Amy. As it was she was damp and cold, and muddy from her frantic struggles. The other two must be freezing in their pantaloons and petticoats but the Frenchmen seemed unaware of their distress.

She wondered where the French cavalrymen were taking them. Would they go all the way to Badajoz? They had left the track to avoid capture in case the British force sent out another patrol but the French must be based somewhere. She wondered how the force that had been sent to fight the French reinforcements was getting on? Would they come across the soldiers still fighting?

They did come across the French, but some distance from where the British attack had taken place. Although Megan's heart sank that they had not passed the returning British on the way, she was gratified to see many walking wounded, and two carts carrying those who were unable to walk. The French battalion plodded its way to Badajoz through the rain that had started to fall, a situation that made the girls' discomfort even worse.

The four Frenchmen who had kidnapped the girls were met with cheers and shouts – a small victory amidst their companions' stunning defeat by the British a short time before. The four basked in the glory of the moment. The girls were pinched and groped. Hands tried to grasp them while they were still on horseback as the men rode towards their own cavalry troop. Megan used her extensive vocabulary learned from the British soldiers and pushed the grabbing hands away. Sarah also spiritedly did so, but poor Amy Rogers timidly shrank away from the teasing men as much as she could.

Megan had a fair knowledge of the French language, taught by her governess and not paid much heed to at the time, but she made an effort to comprehend what their captors were saying and found she could understand a great deal of it. They were boasting of their capture to friends but their jubilation was short-lived when a cavalry Major, hearing the commotion behind him, came riding from somewhere further along the slow column to see what the fuss was about. When he saw the three girls he was furious and told the cavalrymen they were stupid to take female prisoners. "What were you thinking of?" he bellowed in French. "What are we to do with them? Do you think the British will thank us for taking their women? It is bad enough we have lost so many men for the cause this morning. Now you encourage the British to hurry after us again!"

The French lieutenant who rode the same horse as Megan explained that they had already fought off a rescue party which mollified the Major somewhat. "*Bien*! But you had better keep a good eye on them, Pierre," he said to the lieutenant. "If they escape they will tell the British our plans."

"I will keep a good eye, Major. Never fear," replied the lieutenant, turning in the saddle to face Megan and leering at her, his intentions very plain. Megan lifted a hand and slapped his face hard. The man's face twisted into a snarl and he raised his hand to strike her back but the Major stopped him with a sharp word. "Do you not know how to treat a woman, Pierre?" he said. He smiled at Megan and said in good English. "My apologies, *cherie*. Come. You will ride with me." Megan dismounted, knowing she had won a battle of sorts while the French lieutenant's hard, brown eyes glared impotently at her, knowing there was nothing he could do in the face of a senior officer.

The Major helped her up onto his big roan and spoke harshly to Sarah and Amy's captors. "Treat them with respect, and for God's sake give them cloaks to wear!" he ordered before turning his horse and cantering back to his place in the column, leaving a fuming lieutenant and the other two girls even more frightened without Megan's strong presence.

The French column moved slowly on towards Badajoz, its number of fighting men depleted, and now with a number of cavalry watching its back in case of further British attacks. Riding with them, *Teniente* (Lieutenant) Pierre Bordeaux listened to his colleagues' account of the surprise bad turn in their fortunes and seethed with anger at the Major who now had the beautiful English girl on his horse. A handsome man with a long face and high cheek-bones, Bordeaux scowled at his friends who still rode with the girls they had taken. It had been he who had suggested the abduction, riding so close to the British camp and coming across the three girls bathing in the stream. He had immediately been struck by the beauty of the one with chestnut coloured hair and knew he must have her. The danger of being so close to the British, the girls' screams, and racing away with them, had all added spice to the kidnapping – an adventurous interlude in the boring march towards Badajoz and now that damn Major Deneuve had taken the one who so attracted him. It was not to be borne. He cared nothing for the fate of the other two girls but he would have that one. Somehow he would get her back and then she would find out what a French lover was like. He was aristocracy and had had enough of Spanish whores. He put a hand on his cheek where she had slapped him and smiled faintly. A girl with spirit. He liked that, but he would tame her.

There were shouts from up ahead and he realised that his meditations had made him lag behind his fellows. With a sigh he kicked his horse into a canter and fell in behind the Major and his prize so that he could keep them both in sight. It would have to be good enough for now. But later … later would be a different matter.

Chapter 4

The rain was still falling when the two wounded members of the search party finally made it back to the British camp with the dead men's horses. Whilst getting their wounds seen to, the two described the chase to a worried group who had been anxiously awaiting their return, a group that included Will, Richard Camberwell, and Amy Rogers's husband, Joe. That the search party had come back empty-handed made Richard Camberwell's bad temper even worse. This further set-back, worry, and the pain from his broken ankle gave him the disposition of an angry bear and he railed at the two embarrassed soldiers until Lieutenant-Colonel Davenport spoke sharply to him.

"May I remind you, Captain, that this unfortunate incident was brought about by your niece who did not follow orders. She has also unwittingly caused the deaths of three of my men," he snapped. "Now, I suggest you go to your quarters, sir!"

Unrepentant, and after one last reproachful growl, Camberwell allowed Will to help him back to his tent while the battalion's commanding officer dispatched a party to bring in the three men killed by the French kidnappers.

"I should have gone with them, Will," said Camberwell angrily, grimacing and lifting his sore foot onto the cot he was resting on. "The useless bastards might've known the French would set up an ambush."

Although he was just as worried about Megan as his master, and very disappointed that she had not been found, Will felt some sympathy for the search party. "You couldn't go with 'em, sir," he said. "We were away when they left. And like the Colonel said, three men were killed, sir.."

Camberwell scowled. "Damn well deserve to be," he said unfeelingly. "If it was up to me I'd shoot the other two bastards as well." He looked gloomily at his ankle, now encased in splints and bandages. "And this bloody ankle means I can't go after them. We must send another search party."

"I've been thinkin' about that, sir," said Will. "The French'll expect us ter follow 'em." He poured the captain some medicinal brandy. "And they won't be caught out again. They know we're 'ere and I bet they'll be hot-footin' it ter Badajoz by now so they get there before us." He looked at his recumbent master thoughtfully. "But if one person were ter go …" He left the rest of the sentence unsaid.

Camberwell stared back at him, realised what was in the boy's mind, and shook his head. "Oh, no. Don't you think of going yourself," he warned. "I'll speak to the Peer and get a Company to go on ahead of us. The French will be travelling slowly with all their wounded. Maybe a Company could at least keep the bastards in view until we catch up with them." He gazed at his foot again. "Damn this ankle!" He was quiet for a moment, then, "Megan has some French and I trust she will let them know her breeding. If she's lucky enough to have been captured by an officer, she may be able to preserve her virtue until we can rescue her. It's not her I'm worried about so much. It's Sarah. She has nothing to bargain with." He drank some of the brandy, then said, "Go and ask one of the Peer's aids if he can see me, Will. I need to talk to him about this. Davenport says we're leaving tomorrow and I need a party to leave before then. Go on, lad! Quickly now!"

Will did as he was bid and asked if Wellington could see Camberwell at his convenience but all the time he was thinking of Megan and the other two girls. He did not share Richard Camberwell's conviction that French officers had the same moral values as some of the British and he was worried. He determined that even if Wellington agreed to release a Company to go in search of them, he would go alone. That he would be going against his master's orders, and leaving Camberwell to the poor ministrations of Dodge, the elderly man who did the officers' laundry, was not even a consideration. Richard Camberwell must understand that it was something he needed to do. And do it he must. He just hoped that Wellington would not view his absence as desertion, for if he did so, the penalty was death.

*

Early the next morning, Will stood beside a stunted tree, rubbed tired eyes, and stared across a valley. He thought the river he could see flowing through the valley must be the Guadiana but then it could be a tributary as this one was not very wide. He had been told that Badajoz was on the banks of the Guadiana. The air was cold, the sun barely peeping through the clouds overhead. Lightfoot stood still while Will dug in the leather bag that was tied to the saddle and brought out a piece of twice-baked bread that was so hard he was in danger of breaking his teeth as he ate it. That, a large piece of mouldy cheese, and a chunk of tough beef was all the food he had managed to scrounge before leaving the camp in the darkness of the pre-dawn.

Captain Camberwell had finally fallen into a drunken sleep just before midnight, not long after meeting with the General as requested. Wellington had been against sending another search party ahead of the army the next morning, citing the fact that the French would be too far ahead of them by now. This had hardened Will's resolve to go alone. Every minute wasted was a minute Megan was in danger and once he was sure the captain was asleep he had sneaked out of the tent and made his own preparations. Because of his inability to write, he had been unable to leave a note but he had woken his friend George Trim and told him where he was going. George, half asleep, had at first grumbled about being awakened, then sat up in shock as what Will was telling him penetrated his sleepy brain. He remonstrated in loud whispers.

"Will! Yer can't go alone. What if yer run into the French?"

"That's what I 'ope ter do." Will said. "Look. The more time we sit 'ere, the more chance we'll 'ave 've not getting the girls back. I 'ave ter go, George. I 'ave ter!"

George thought back to the girl he had left at home, and nodded. He could understand his friend's concern, but he didn't look forward to informing Richard Camberwell in the morning and almost wished Will had gone without telling him. "The Captain'll be furious," he said.

"I know, but I need fer you ter tell 'im so's 'e knows I 'aven't deserted," Will insisted. "Tell 'im I'll meet up with 'im at Badajoz." Will hoped that he would be able to do so.

The journey so far had been cold and damp. Now he tossed the hard bread crust to Scrapper who lay patiently at Lightfoot's feet. He had tried to leave the dog behind but Scrapper had had enough of his new master going off and leaving him and had set up such a whining that Will was scared someone would hear and investigate, so he had reluctantly let him come along. It was easy for someone of Will's expertise to evade the sleepy sentries and the pouring rain helped to hide the sound of Lightfoot's hooves. He had changed into civilian clothes. He had even taken off his hated boots though he had them in the bag with the food. Once changed, with an old woollen hat hiding his thatch of blond hair, he looked like a peasant boy, though his blue eyes would have given him away to anyone taking a close look. He had wanted to take his rifle but it would immediately give away the fact that he was a British soldier, so he had reluctantly left it behind with George. Instead, he had stolen a kitchen knife from the cook tent. It made him feel better to at least have a weapon of sorts should he run into any of the enemy as he hoped to do.

The rain had stopped with the dawn, and daylight, together with incriminating horse dung, wheel tracks and many footprints, told Will that he was on the trail of the French army, though there was no sign yet of any soldiers. He sent Lightfoot down the slope and followed the river south. Soon, however, he saw thin skeins of smoke on the horizon and judged by their number that they came from the enemy's morning camp-fires. He stopped, not eager to get too close. There was nothing he could do by himself while the French reinforcements marched. At the moment it would be enough just to make sure that Megan and the girls were all right. He found a sheltered spot inside a small stand of trees, tied Scrapper to one as his guard, and caught up on some of the sleep he had lost the night before.

When he awoke, the morning was well on and it was a little warmer when the scudding clouds didn't hide the sun. He threw off the thin blanket and rummaged in his bag for the meat, sharing it with Scrapper who was pleased his master was moving around again. He barked at Will, hurrying him along, satisfied only when Will was once again in the saddle and ready to go. Considering the dog had only three good legs he kept up pretty well, Will thought as they went steadily along the track. Scrapper's bandage had come off twice already because of his antics and he sometimes tried to bite it, as though it irritated him, but he certainly did not let his bad leg stop him getting about. Will also thought of Richard Camberwell and he felt a small pang of guilt and apprehension. That the captain would be angry was an understatement – he would be furious. Not only because Will had gone alone, but because he would now have to put up with Dodge looking after him while his ankle mended. At least he had not taken Hades, Will pondered, though the thought had crossed his mind because she was a much faster horse than Lightfoot, but Will had fallen back on the sturdy Welsh cob because of her ponderous and gentle ways. Although he knew Hades well he did not feel confident enough to cope with riding him over long distances. The horse's temperament bore a remarkable similarity to that of his master. He tried to imagine Camberwell's rage if he had stolen the horse as well as leaving him to Dodge's ministrations, and shook his head, laughing, glad that he had not given in to the temptation.

Another hour and he passed the site of the French encampment. The enemy had not stayed there long, only enough time to get a few hours' sleep by the look of it, and to eat a quick morning meal. Probably too scared of being followed by the British, Will supposed. He wondered how far it was to Badajoz and what he would do when he got there. His plans had gone no further than following the French. After that he thought he would have to play it by ear. He thought of being alone in a French-held city, but it wasn't fear that made his heart beat faster. It was excitement.

He spent another cold night in the open with only Scrapper lying next to him for warmth and the French fires in the distance. He did not get much sleep, afraid of French patrols that might be scouting for the British who must, by now, be hot on the trail of the enemy. The British would be slow because of the army's size, its baggage train, and the number of camp followers, but might be moving at a faster pace than the French with all their wounded. He wondered if it would be better for him to be closer to the French or closer to the British. There were down sides to both at the moment.

He was on the move again before dawn having decided that he needed to catch up with the French. Before sleep had claimed him the night before, he had formed a daring plan. Rescuing Megan and the girls would not be an option while the French were marching, so he needed to get into Badajoz and, once there, he would perhaps be able to find out where they were being held captive. He had puzzled for some time as to how he would achieve entry into the town before an idea had come to him, but it was dangerous and if it did not work, could easily lead to his capture, or worse.

The French had not long left their overnight camp when Will passed it by and he knew he was getting close. He remembered Richard Camberwell saying they were not too far from Badajoz when back at the British camp and he expected to reach the fortress that day. Before he had gone far, the sky darkened and the rain came again, pelting down in streams, so that Lightfoot plodded along the muddy track even more slowly, and Scrapper slunk beside him with wet tail dragging, and limping badly. Will was content not to try and speed them up, knowing that the bad weather would also slow down the French. The mud would cling to cartwheels and artillery limbers and make any sort of meaningful progress difficult. As it was, Lightfoot just seemed to keep going steadily and he was sure he would soon catch up with the enemy's rear.

He was right. He heard the French army before he saw them. Some of the men were singing, a deep bellow of sound. Will had never seen the French attacking on a battlefield but Richard Camberwell had told him that they attacked in massive columns of men, and that their war-cry was "*Vive l'Empereur!*" When that huge sound drifted across a plain, it sent fear into the hearts of the British. Will supposed that the men were singing now to keep their spirits up in the rain, but as he got closer he could also hear shouts and women's voices. He left Lightfoot at the bottom of a hill and climbed the sodden grass to the top and there -at last- he saw the French reinforcing army, marching slowly in the clinging mud.

Then his attention was taken away from the French for in the distance was a far more imposing sight. The river he had been following was the Guadiana after all, for there, beside it, was the fortress of Badajoz. Will stared at the city that the British army was coming to besiege and knew, in that moment, that Wellington must be crazy. He had thought Ciudad Rodrigo huge and difficult but it was nothing to Badajoz. Facing him on a hill was a castle and, to the left of it, two of the crenellated forts that stuck out of the high walls. To his right, on the other side of the river and separate from the city, were two more. Richard Camberwell had told him that the south side of the town had several forts built into the walls. If they, and the castle, were all manned with French artillery, Will could not see how the British could possibly break through as every side was protected. It was an impossible task. Will had every faith in the army he belonged to and was proud to be a part of it, but he could not possibly imagine any army being big enough or strong enough to penetrate those defences.

The rain was easing a bit, but he was already soaked so it made little difference. Glancing at the wet, blue-coated French soldiers he saw some cavalry riding back towards the stragglers at the rear of the column and he stared at a head of bedraggled chestnut hair on a figure behind one of the riders. It was Megan, wearing a soldier's cloak.

His first instinct was to shout, then to run down the hillside towards her, but common sense made him do neither. He watched, his heart pounding, as the cavalry officer made his brown mare step close to a woman who was struggling with bags and two small children right at the back of the column. The man appeared to be shouting at her but then Will saw Megan say something to him. They appeared to be arguing, then the man spoke to the woman and she lifted the smallest child into Megan's arms. A pang of jealousy ran through Will as he watched her seat the child in front of her, wrap one arm around her waist, and the other around the horseman's before he cantered back to his place in the column.

The incident reminded Will of his plan and he waited until the stragglers had gone around the next bend then he slid back down the hillside to

Lightfoot, Scrapper hopping and scrabbling after him. He mounted Lightfoot and sent the cob at a fast trot to catch up with the French. As he did so, he thought back to what he had seen. Megan, it seemed, was safe enough for now and he assumed the other two girls were too. It appeared, as well, that she was not too worried about her immediate welfare and that she seemed to have some rapport of a sort with her captor. That thought brought another pang of jealousy but he tried to suppress it, knowing that Megan would do well not to antagonize her kidnappers, though it would surprise him if she did not, knowing her as he did. Megan and Richard Camberwell had similar temperaments and he knew Megan well enough to know that she would have resisted capture as much as possible. Maybe she had decided that acquiescence was the best policy for the time being.

Will caught up with the tail end of the slow French column as they rounded a bend in the track and came within sight of Badajoz. The camp followers, baggage handlers, wounded in the carts, and traders that accompanied the enemy paid no attention when Will pulled Lightfoot to a halt and joined them as they stood and stared at the fortified city ahead. There was a buzz of excited conversation which Will did not understand at all, though he assumed that they were relieved to have arrived. He and Scrapper stood next to the woman with the small child who had been lagging behind a short time before and saw her pointing out the defences to her son. She smiled and sounded happy, pulling at the arm of a friend and talking in fast French. Will felt strangely alien. He understood only a few words of the language and he wondered at his own audacity in mingling with the enemy like this, but he could think of no other way in which to enter the town. However, despite the fact that everyone's attention was taken by the huge edifice before them, he took care not to draw attention to himself. A short distance away he saw a mule piled high with forage for the cavalry horses. One of the bundles was slipping off the back of the beast so while the muleteer was otherwise engrossed in staring at the castle, Will crept up and unfastened the bundle, then quickly tied it onto Lightfoot's back. This had the double advantage of making it look like the cob was part of the baggage train, and it partially hid Will from any prying eyes, though he was careful to keep his own face averted from anyone's direct gaze. If someone noticed his bright blue eyes they would know immediately that he was not the Spanish peasant boy he was pretending to be. Scrapper, excited by the throng, barked, and twisted his thin body between people's legs. Will, worried that this might invite unwelcome attention, admonished him sharply and the dog reluctantly settled down at his feet.

The column in front started to move and the women and children walked on with a spring in their steps now that they were at last close to shelter and food. The chatter increased the nearer they came to the high, thick walls, thronged with French soldiers who cheered the arrival of reinforcements. All knew that the British were not far behind this battalion. Will smiled and cheered with the rest of them when the big gates opened to receive the French force, a force battered by the British assault a few days before, but ready and willing to seek revenge on their enemies from the safety of the huge fortress.

The gates creaked slowly shut behind him as Will walked into the stronghold, leading Lightfoot and with Scrapper at his heels. Once out of sight of the sentries on the wall he took a different direction and let the French column go on without him. He was in. In Badajoz, the great Spanish stronghold that was in the hands of the French. Now it was up to him to find Megan and the others. Seeing a narrow alleyway that looked obligingly empty, he stopped and let the excitement grip him. In his mind he was no longer a soldier, but a street urchin again as he had been in London Town all those months ago. He forgot Wellington and Richard Camberwell, forgot that he was in all probability branded a deserter. For now he was just Will Tucker, a boy with no home but plenty of street savvy. This was a town just like any other. It might be filled with French soldiers and Spanish civilians and he was probably the only Englishman in the whole place, but he would blend in and he would find his girl, even if it meant dying in the attempt. Because he could not stand by and let the French have her. Megan was everything to him. He loved her and he would get her back.

Chapter 5

Megan Camberwell clung to the child pressed tightly against her stomach and looked about her with nervous excitement. The horses trotted along cobbled and dirt streets, some of the houses that pressed in from either side were quite good, others little more than hovels. She glanced at Sarah and Amy riding with their captors a short distance in front and wondered if they were thinking the same thoughts. What was to become of them? Why had they been captured? It appeared to have been a spontaneous action by the French lieutenant that had taken them away from the British camp. She hoped that they would be exchanged for French prisoners, but that was by no means a certainty. It was possible that the officer had no other purpose than to abuse them. Megan knew that men found her desirable. Had she not found that out already? There had been those two farm labourers she and Will had met on their way to Portsmouth and then all the trouble with Lieutenant Paul Deaville only a few short weeks before. Both incidents had nearly been her undoing and if it had not been for Will she would not still have her virginity intact. The thought of Will almost brought tears to her eyes and she wished above all things that he was with her now.

They passed by a cathedral, a huge edifice that took up one side of a plaza and she wondered that Spain could be so poor, and yet they had the money to build such a thing. The citizens she could see, few because of the rain that still fell, seemed to take no notice of the men and horses that had marched into their city and she wondered what it would be like to live in a place taken over by strangers. She supposed people would try to get on with their lives as best they could. She thought back to Ciudad Rodrigo and remembered the terrible aftermath of the British victory. The soldiers had behaved like crazed beasts; drinking themselves senseless, whoring and looting as though their lives depended on it, but Will had told her it was the soldiers' way. They put their lives at such a risk to gain victory, that they considered the women, drink and contents of the town they had fought for, their just reward. It was something she thought she would never understand. She had come to know some of the soldiers well in the last few months. Her friend, Ginny Makepiece, a woman whose kind heart had done a lot to help Megan come to terms with army life, had a husband who was a sergeant, a sensible, friendly man whom others admired and respected, yet she had heard that he had been as drunk as the rest, and had brought all sorts of trinkets stolen out of the town for his wife and family after the siege.

The horse she was on stopped and Megan's attention was brought back to her immediate situation. Major Francois Deneuve shouted orders to some of the infantry and then dismounted.

"*Parlez-vous Francais?*" he asked her.

"*Oui.* I learned French at school," she told him.

"*Tres bien.* Very good," he said, and told her to get down. She handed the child to its grateful mother who had followed them this far, and dismounted while the officer shouted to the troopers who held her friends to bring the girls to him.

"When we are settled, I will speak with you," Deneuve said as Sarah and Amy hurried over to her, eager to be with their friend again. Both girls, frightened at their sudden change of circumstances, looked to her for a lead. Sarah, although confident when dealing with the wounded, and spirited enough to have stowed away on the ship that had brought them here, was nervous, and Amy a wreck. They listened now as the imposing officer shouted instructions to his men. Sarah, schooled by a friend of her father's, had a smattering of French. It was thought necessary to learn the language as her father was a well-to-do merchant with sensible foresight who hoped that one day the British government would find it within its power to trade with the French instead of fighting them. Lacking a son, he had had high hopes that Sarah, being a brighter than average daughter, would some day take an interest in his business and had insisted that French be one of her accomplishments. Thus she understood now that the girls would be accommodated in a house the Major intended to take from one of the town's folk for himself and other officers. This disturbed all three girls, not knowing what the officers' intentions would be. The lieutenant who had captured Megan was with the group and the looks he kept sending in her direction could only be described as lascivious. The cavalry troopers who had captured them looked sorry to be giving up Sarah and Amy to officers and Sarah heard one of them comment, while he watched a fat Spanish matron hurrying down the street, that it wasn't fair how the officers always got the cream while they were left with the sour milk.

The Major took the girls to a large nearby house that stood on its own within a walled garden. It showed it was unoccupied by French troops due to the lack of letters and numbers on the wall by the gate, a system the

British used as well to signify which regiment, battalion and the number of men who were in residence. The Frenchman shouldered the cringing owner of the house out of the way when he opened the door, thrust aside his wife and three small children and demanded in a mixture of French and Spanish that the family must get out or be shot as enemies of Napoleon. The family got the message but scarcely had time to gather a few belongings before they were pushed out into the rain, the woman crying and wailing, her children staring wide-eyed at the men who had invaded their home. The three English girls were taken upstairs to a bedroom and told that this was where they would stay.

"A guard will be outside the door at all times, *mademoiselles*," said the Major, an unfriendly smile twitching his black moustache. "So do not think of trying to escape. I have plans for you."

What the plans were, he did not say. The door closed behind him and the three looked at each other for a moment before Amy Rogers sat down heavily on the rough wooden bed and burst into tears. She howled so loudly that Megan went to her and shook her hard.

"Amy! Stop that bloody noise! Crying will not do us any good at all! Be quiet now, for God's sake!" she demanded and the girl, so startled by her friend's sharp voice and swearing, blubbered to a halt.

"But Megan, what are we to do?" she said.

"I don't know yet, but for sure crying will not help!" said Megan sharply. She sat down beside Amy with Sarah on her other side. Megan was quiet for a few minutes while she thought, the silence of the room interspersed with orders being shouted, the sound of horses' hooves on the cobbles of the yard outside and Amy's sniffs, then she said firmly, "I think we are worth more to them as bargaining pieces. We will tell them we are aristocrats. Our relations are lords, and our husbands are officers and they will be willing to pay to get us back unharmed when the French win the battle."

Amy Rogers stared at her in amazement. She was a small girl, thin and plain, married at fifteen to one of the corporals in B Company when his own wife had died in childbirth. The man, ten years older, had nearly worn her out with his nightly exploits after Ciudad Rodrigo and she believed she was pregnant, a condition that she had told no one about and scared her to bits. Now she did. She told her two friends that she had missed two of those irritating times of the month and what was she to do without the help of women like Ginny Makepiece when her time came and why was Megan so sure that the French would win the forthcoming battle?

Megan gave her a scornful look. "Silly girl! Of course the British will win, but we must make these damn bastards think that they will be the victors if we are to be safe. And don't worry about the baby coming, we won't be here by then. My uncle will come for us when the army breaches the walls." She said this more confidently than she felt but she knew that it was important to keep their hopes of rescue alive. She smiled at Amy who smiled tremulously back. Amy Rogers knew that Megan Camberwell was a young lady of forceful temperament, but her language! It was as bad as that used in the tenement in which she had grown up. Why hadn't her uncle said something to her about it? It was said that Lady Camberwell made a habit of using strong language all the time. However, Megan's words had lifted her spirits and she did not feel quite so bad about the situation with Megan and Sarah, whose quiet strength in the hospital wards at Ciudad Rodrigo was well known, beside her.

They heard footsteps and Megan hushed the other two. "Let me do the talking," she whispered. Sarah had taken the time to discard the soaked cloaks and to wrap herself and Amy in a couple of blankets. Both were freezing and wet, being as they were only dressed in their underwear and they shivered with cold as much as apprehension when the Major strode into the room.

"This will do us very nicely," he said, smiling and rubbing his hands together as though he too were cold. Either that or very pleased about something. Megan suspected it was the latter, and that they were the cause of the officer's good humour. "Now, *mademoiselles*. What to do with you, eh? That is the question. It was stupid of Pierre to bring you along, but now you are here, what are we to do?"

He stared at the three and the smile broadened, though it did not reach his eyes. He was a large, fleshy man, dressed in the uniform of the French *Chasseurs a Cheval,* the Light Horse, dark green tunic with white lace, and the same colour overalls with high black boots. He put a hand in his pocket and brought out the stub of a cigar that he lit from the nearly dead fire spluttering in the grate. There were logs beside it and he threw a couple on, making small flames lick around the wood and the girls were glad of the sudden warmth. "Cannot have you dying of cold now, can we?" he said.

"Would have been nice if you'd thought of that before," muttered Megan.

If the Major heard, he ignored the comment. He stood in front of the fire and warmed his backside, successfully keeping the heat from the girls. He stared at them thoughtfully, thinking that for all his thoughtlessness in capturing them, Pierre Bordeaux had good taste. The one with the chestnut curls was a beauty and the tall one had a fey prettiness. The small girl was plain, but he knew a few officers who would like her daintiness. Their presence caused him a problem though. He guessed that at least two of them belonged to officers and they would be angry at their disappearance. Pierre had told him that they had been chased, though this time the French had been the victors of that small skirmish. But if, though it was highly unlikely, the British ever entered the town, no mercy would be shown for the kidnappers. For the moment the girls were safe, but … He scratched his chin thoughtfully. Maybe there was money to be made here. Francois Deneuve had been in the army a long time but he liked the good life; good wines and brandy, excellent food and, of course, fine women. He would take the beauty for himself. It would be a snub to the British and he knew he could subdue that waywardness he had already seen in her when she had demanded that they take the child from the woman who was lagging behind the column on the march. But maybe there was more to be had here than mere pleasure. He asked for their names and if they had husbands.

"My name is Lady Megan Camberwell and my husband is a Lord," Megan answered imperiously. "And the Captain of a Light Company." This Major Deneuve could believe. The girl was dressed in a simple brown dress that had obviously seen many better days, but there was an air of authority about her, and a flash of fire in those hazel eyes. He saw the other two girls glance at her as she continued. "My friend's husband is a Major in my husband's regiment, and this one …" she gestured towards Amy who was looking at her with eyes that expressed admiration for her blatant lies, "this girl is promised to a lieutenant. We are all of good birth, Major, and none of our men will be pleased by your shocking behaviour in bringing us here. We wish to be released at once!"

Deneuve laughed loudly. The girl had spirit, and he liked that in a woman. "Now what do you suppose your British officers are going to do, my lady?" he said in an amused tone. "Here we are in Badajoz which, if rumour is to be believed, will soon be besieged by your forces. Certainly no one from your side will be allowed in and we have enough men and guns to see off Wellington's paltry army." He swept his arm to encompass the room and beyond. "This place is impregnable. We have men in all the forts and the castle; a ditch that is more than twenty feet deep; the walls of the city are fifty feet high and the castle to the north is built on a hundred feet of rock with a forty foot wall above that. There are around five thousand French men here and enough guns to cover every side of the city. Do you really think that your dear husbands will be in a position to come and rescue you?" He laughed again, derisively. "They will die, my dear. They will die like the rest of the scum you call an army."

For an instant Megan paled at his words, as did the other two girls, but then her fierce temper took over, and she ran towards the smug Frenchman, beating him with her fists and nearly toppling him into the fire which now blazed merrily behind him. Surprised, he tried to side-step as she flailed at him and shouted that he was a liar, that Wellington's army was the best in the world, and that he had no idea what they could accomplish. Somehow he managed to grab hold of her arms and angrily pushed her backwards, then slapped her hard on the face. The slap stopped her, and she stood, breathing heavily and clutching her smarting cheek, trying desperately not to give him the satisfaction of seeing her cry, for the smack had hurt.

"You will stay here and I will send you some food." There was no amusement in the Major's voice now. It was hard and unyielding. "I will respect the fact that you are officers' ladies, if indeed you all are, but some of my men may not. Beware of upsetting them or you may find yourselves lying on your backs in the gutter."

With that, he left them, and Megan sat down on the bed, her hand still holding her cheek. Sarah sat beside her and put a comforting arm about her waist while Amy started to cry again softly. The girls said nothing, each one occupied with her own thoughts, and none of them optimistic about their future.

Chapter 6

Will soon found out that Badajoz was a dangerous place to be. French troops were everywhere. Spanish civilians scurried around like frightened chickens. They had heard, as had the French, that the British were on their way to besiege the city and many had fled, leaving their property to whoever the victors happened to be.

The first thing Will had to do was to put Lightfoot somewhere safe. The horse that had been a great help in getting him here was now a liability because he had no hope of keeping a low profile with the cob in tow. He followed a horse and cart and found a carter on the outskirts of the city, near the city wall. Watching from a short distance he ascertained that the man kept several horses. He wondered what would be the best thing to do. An idea came to him but it would mean stealing again. Still – what of that? He could rationalise it by thinking he was doing it for Megan, for whom he would do anything in the world.

He wandered until he came to a more affluent part of town. Few of the regular inhabitants lived here still, most having fled with their valuables when they had the chance, but he did come to a house that was apparently occupied by several French officers. He had no compunction about stealing from them, and remembered the occasion when he had stolen money from one of his future Company officers back in Portsmouth. Tying Lightfoot to a tree and bidding Scrapper to lie down and be quiet, he watched and waited his chance. It came sooner than expected, but not in the way he had envisaged.

A carriage drew up outside the house. It had been there for maybe twenty minutes when the door opened and three women came out. They were chattering in shrill, high voices and, judging by their painted faces and low-cut bodices, Will thought they were probably whores hired by the French officers. They minced down the short driveway, conversing in Spanish, laughing, and seemingly in very high spirits. They must have been summoned from a high class brothel for them to have transport at their beck and call, thought Will, watching them approach the carriage. Two of the women climbed in but as the third lifted her foot to climb the steps, she tripped on the hem of her dress and went sprawling on the cobbles.

The woman shrieked and there followed a great fuss as she tried to gather herself together, the other two remonstrating with the carriage driver who looked on with disdain, obviously not prepared to help. Will paid little attention. He had seen a much more arresting sight than dirty bloomers. The woman must have had a small purse about her person because that purse was now under the carriage, half hidden behind a wheel. He prayed the woman would not notice and it seemed she did not because once she was on her feet and had straightened her dress, she climbed into the carriage rubbing her knee and cursing the driver loudly.

The carriage drove off and Will looked up and down the road to make sure there was no one about. The only people he could see were a file of French soldiers turning into the street, but they were far enough away not to notice him when he ran from his hiding place and swiftly picked up the purse. Within seconds he was back with Lightfoot and Scrapper, the purse a comforting weight tucked into his shirt, and thanking his lucky stars that he had witnessed the small accident.

Will went back to the carter with the idea to spin him a story that he worked for a nobleman who had to stay in Badajoz because he had nowhere else to go. He would say that the French had taken the nobleman's best horses but left this one pony. However, he was worried that this too would be stolen by the besieging British if they should take over the town, so he would like the carter to look after him until the threatened siege was over. Relaying this to the carter was not easy due to Will's minimal Spanish but at least he managed to make the man understand that he had money and that the carter should look after the horse. Will had also worried that his blue eyes would give him away as an Englishman but either the carter had poor eyesight, or he did not care, and the discrepancy was not remarked upon. Maybe he thinks I'm with the French army, Will reflected as the man's dark eyes stared at the coins Will took out of the purse. They seemed to be all that the man was interested in, so Will was very relieved when the man patted Lightfoot and indicated that he would look after the horse. A pleasant, if avaricious, man with time on his hands, he chattered on and Will, catching the gist of what he was saying, understood that he had only managed to keep his horses by promising the French officer who had tried to commandeer them that he would use his carts to transport the dead to a burial site when the battle was done, a job that no one usually volunteered for. He was glad of the money and said he would do his best to see that Lightfoot remained in his care.

Pleased that he had managed to see that Lightfoot was all right, and still with a little of the whore's money in his pocket, Will furtively walked around Badajoz with Scrapper at his side, taking in everything he saw. He learned nothing of the girls' whereabouts but spent the hours trying to keep away from French patrols that were hurrying Spanish citizens off the streets before nightfall. As dusk fell he wondered what to do next. He slipped into a fetid alleyway and leaned against the wall. He was hungry and tired. Scrapper lay down at his feet as though he felt the same. The dog had been another problem. He tended to draw attention to Will when he least needed it and growled protectively if anyone came too close, but Will thought the dog would at least not arouse anyone's suspicions, whereas Lightfoot would have done. It would not be considered normal for a street urchin to be the owner of a horse and it would be assumed that he had stolen it.

Will heard voices, laughter, and the sound of hooves on the cobbled street outside the alley. He peered out, putting his hand on Scrapper's head to stop him running out at the horses, then his heart jumped as he recognised one of the riders. Coming towards the alley was a group of French officers and leading them was the Major who had shared a horse with Megan. Will squinted in the half-light, not sure at first that it was he. Most of the Frenchmen had moustaches and looked alike to him, and the dusk made it difficult to see. He leaned further out, wishing he had brought his rifle with him. The only weapon he had was the knife. Then a thought struck him. If he could only follow the officer, he could maybe find out where the girls were.

Suddenly a shrill voice shrieked indignant Spanish behind him and Scrapper started to bark. Thoughts of following the French officers fled as Will was made aware of the imminent danger of discovery. He turned swiftly and saw a boy outlined darkly in a half open doorway that he had not noticed in the black wall. Immediately Will grabbed hold of him and put a dirty hand over his mouth, at the same time hissing at both boy and dog to shut up and pushing himself and them backwards through the door. Whether the struggling boy understood English or not, he stared up at Will with defiant black eyes, but was quiet.

The street outside was quiet too, and Will's heart thumped madly against his chest as he waited, knowing that the boy's yell had attracted the Frenchmen. The voices and hoofbeats had stopped. Scrapper moved against his leg and the door post as though to get in front of him but Will pressed hard against the dog's side to stop him. Nobody moved. Then a soldier shouted something to his comrades, who laughed, and the horses carried on down the street.

Will breathed again, hardly aware that he had been holding his breath. He let go of the boy and pushed him further inside the house, kicking the door shut behind him. He found himself in a room lit only by the faint light of dusk that came from a dirty window. Scrapper set up a frantic barking again, the hair on his back standing up as he surveyed the child and the other occupants of the room. The room smelled of dirt and urine and boiled vegetables, and something else that sent Will's mind flying back to when he was a boy in London. Extreme poverty.

Though the room was dark, Will could just about make out three other people in the room besides himself and the boy. He was wondering how to introduce himself when the boy he had grabbed spoke a stream of Spanish, pointing at Will and gesticulating to the other occupants of the room. Will realised that Scrapper was still barking and gave a sharp command that he had taught the dog to quieten him. Scrapper gave a last growl and was quiet, but it was obvious from his stance that he was ready to protect Will from any attack.

One of the gloomy figures stood up and lit a candle, the flickering flame throwing black shadows into the furthest corners of the room. By its light Will was surprised to see that all the people in the room were children. The boy who had startled him in the alley looked to be about ten years old, thin and wiry, with a shock of black hair. There was a girl, a couple of years younger, her long black hair tangled, her face pinched and wan. An older girl held a baby of about a year. It was hard to tell the older girl's age. She could have been anywhere between twelve and sixteen, and had a thin face like her sister – a face that would be pretty if clean, Will thought. She stared at Will with big frightened eyes, seeming as dumb as the small girl and the baby who had a thumb in its mouth, but then she suddenly broke the silence that had followed the boy's tirade.

"Who are you?" she asked in Spanish, her voice barely above a whisper.

Will's knowledge of the language was sparse but he understood. "My name's Will," he said. "I'm English."

The girl's eyes widened further and the boy spat on the floor before making a derisive comment. The girl hushed him with a sharp word.

"What are you doing 'ere? 'As the army come? What do you want with us?" she asked in halting English.

"No, the army's still on its way. I won't 'urt yer. I'm alone," Will answered.

"I'm lookin' fer someone." He looked around the dingy room, at the two filthy mattresses on the floor, the cooking pot hanging over a small fireplace in which a couple of logs smoked, and the dirty pile of clothing in a corner. "Are yer by yerselves? Is there no one ter take care of yer?"

The girl looked blankly at him, but with mime and a mixture of Spanish and English as he repeated the questions, Will finally made her understand. She shook her head sadly. "The French, they kill our parents. They were big people in Badajoz." By that Will understood her to mean they had been well-to-do, maybe even part of the ruling elite. "The French, they leave us to look for ourselves," the girl continued. She spread her hand to encompass the other children. "I look for them."

Will surveyed the small family with compassion. They were dressed in what may once have been good clothing but now their clothes were unwashed and the boy's showed signs of wear and tear. The two younger children had runny noses. Will guessed that the boy was probably the main provider and he well knew what it was like to have to beg and scavenge for food. But to have to feed a family – that would be ten times more difficult than the life he had led in London when he had had only himself to think about.

The small girl, who until then had said nothing at all but had gazed at Will with frightened eyes and held onto her sister's skirt, wiped her nose on the back of a dirty sleeve and pointed to Scrapper who was lying down quite comfortably now that he realised Will was in no danger from these strangers. His tongue hung out and he panted and this obviously amused the child for she smiled and looked up at her big sister. She pointed to her own mouth, then at the dog. The older girl smiled back, then said to Will. "Rosa, she think your dog laughs. It is good that my sister is 'appy. She 'as not spoken since the French kill Mama and Papa. We 'ave not much laughter."

Will stared at the small girl who was watching Scrapper with rapt attention while still clinging to her sister's skirt. He crouched down and beckoned her to come to him. The girl's big brown eyes gazed at him, then she looked at her sister. The older girl smiled and nodded. Slowly the little girl walked towards Will and took his hand. Will carefully placed the small palm on Scrapper's fur and helped her to stroke his back. Scrapper stood still while the child stroked him. The girl smiled.

Watching them, an idea came to Will. This room would make an ideal hiding place for himself and Scrapper while he continued his search for Megan and the others. He remembered the money in his pocket and took out the purse. The two older children stared at it as though he had just done a magic trick. "I 'ave money," he said. "I'll buy food if yer let me stay 'ere for a while." The girl looked troubled. "What is it?" he asked, puzzled. He thought she would have been pleased by his offer "I can 'elp yer," he added.

"*Sí*, that is good," she said. "But there is no food to buy. The French … they 'ave taken it."

Will nodded in understanding. But Badajoz must be full of supplies. The French commissary was notoriously bad at getting through to the army, due mostly to the Partisans and British patrols, but the French would have commandeered food supplies within the city, heedless of the needs of its citizens, another reason why many had left. He smiled and the eldest girl frowned at him, not understanding why her comment should have caused him amusement. "I will get food," he said confidently. It would not take him long to find out where the supplies were being stored and he was confident that he would be able to steal some. Maybe with the help of the boy who was presumably no novice. He had managed to keep his family alive so far.

Will sat on the floor beside the little girl and stroked Scrapper who now seemed quite at home. In a mixture of English, Spanish, and mime, he told the children that he had lived on the streets when he was younger, that he had been forced to find food and shelter wherever he could, and that he had been a pick-pocket. The children's eyes rounded as the tale unfolded, and the shadows grew darker as the night drew in. Finally he was able to make them understand that he would steal if necessary to feed them and himself. The eldest girl, whose name was Maria, asked him why he was in Badajoz and he told her he was looking for friends who had been captured by the French. This sobered her. "It is danger 'ere, Will. You will get caught and the French will kill you." Tears filled her eyes. "Like they did Mama and Papa."

"I will try not ter let that 'appen, Maria," Will answered softly. He turned to the young boy. "You and I will go tomorrow and find food, Juan," he said.

"I go myself," said the boy, sullenly. He had listened to the story with a mutinous expression, and Will thought he knew exactly what the problem was. Since the death of their parents he had been the breadwinner, the man of the house, and now this stranger, this interloper, had come and taken over. "I will 'elp yer, Juan. Yer nearly a man, but yer sister Rosa is too small, and Maria must look after the baby. Won't it be better if there're two pairs of 'ands ter carry food back fer yer family?" He waited, watching the youngster as he thought about what Will had said. Finally the boy nodded slowly. "Maybe," he said. "We will try it for one day."

Will nodded. "One day," he agreed. He dug into the leather bag that he had taken from Lightfoot's saddle before leaving the horse with the carter. There were still a few remnants of food inside. Although he was hungry himself, he gave them to the children who ate the bread and cheese ravenously without a word, though the eldest girl smiled her thanks. "Now I must sleep," he said when they had finished. Maria immediately gave her baby sister to the other girl and dug out a blanket from the pile of clothes in the corner but Will shook his head. He pointed to the dog. "'E's my blanket," he said, and lay down beside the dog who raised his head and looked at him for a few seconds, then contentedly lay down again. The girl busied herself setting out two blankets on the dirty mattresses. The little girl, Rosa, refused to lie with her sister, but lay down on Scrapper's other side. For some time, Will lay sleepless, thinking that maybe he should have gone out to see what pickings he could find tonight, but the rain had started again and he could hear it pouring from the eaves. No one would be out on a night like this except the sentries. No. He and Juan would go in the morning. Searching for food, and news of Megan. Listening to the even breathing of his new friends, he finally fell asleep.

Chapter 7

The British army arrived at Badajoz the following day, 16th March 1812, amid pouring rain. Captain Richard Camberwell, riding Hades at the head of his Light Company, surveyed the wet city as they approached it and his heart fell. The sight of the castle and the eight bastions built into the walls filled him with a cold dread. Since Ciudad Rodrigo, the army had been high-spirited, full of confidence in themselves and their abilities, but this sight was enough to make even the most optimistic man down-hearted. From what he could see, the castle walls and the bastions that surrounded the city bristled with sentries and gun emplacements, and he supposed that the ones he could not see would not be similarly fortified. He looked both east and west and saw there were outlying forts as well, all able to fire on attackers. No doubt there would be a ditch, and a glacis, a high wall of earth, and maybe even a *chevaux de frise*, a wooden beam spiked through with sword blades. All enough to stop a determined attack. And any breach they made would probably be mined. It was impossible to think that anyone, not even an army as good as the one he belonged to, could breach those high walls and take the city.

Camberwell realised that the sight before them, especially with the weather being so foul, must also be making the rank and file despondent and he wondered if there would be deserters before the day was done. Deserters were rare in Britain's army because the penalty, if caught, was hanging, but all must be wondering at the temerity and foolishness of the generals, especially Wellington, in thinking that they could ever overcome Badajoz.

As Hades walked slowly with the other officers' horses towards the city, a hush came over the army. Men who a short time before had been talking amongst themselves as they marched, were quiet as Badajoz revealed itself in all its formidable glory. The only sounds were the rain, the jingle of harness and the creaking roll of wagon wheels as the army marched. The soldiers left the Guadiana river that passed the city to the north-west, and followed, instead, the Rivillas, a small tributary that ran south. They by-passed the dam the French had made, flooding the ground to the east to further protect the city, and finally came to a halt some distance beyond the Rivillas stream. It stood between them and the walled forts that jutted out towards the men like aggressive bull-dogs, massive and wide, the crenellations like huge teeth ready to bite the paltry army that dared to lay seige.

Wellington, his staff, and many of the senior officers rode further to the west and set up headquarters in the small town of Elvas, just across the border in Portugal, and a few miles from Badajoz. The General wondered if the supply lines he had set up to bring food, guns, and ammunition from Lisbon and all parts of Spain for the army now outside Badajoz's walls would get through. British soldiers protected the peasants' mule trains and wagons but Wellington knew that Marshall Soult wanted supplies. His French army was starving in the mountains to the south and he would have patrols scouring the countryside for food. A British baggage train would be like manna from heaven to the French.

Wanting to be closer to the action with his men, and despite the discomforts he knew he would have to endure, Richard Camberwell decided that he would stay with the bulk of the army to the east of Badajoz. He ordered Dodge to set up his tent and make camp, his already bad mood worsening because Will was not there to do it for him.

Will was a sore point with him at the moment. That he had gone to rescue Megan, Sarah, and Amy was not in doubt. Camberwell had heard the news from a very wary George Trim several hours after Will had gone, and he had given the young man a severe tongue lashing for not having informed him straight away. He cursed Will, in his absence, for foolhardiness. Squinting through the driving rain to the spires and domes that could be seen above the city walls, he wondered if the boy was even now inside the city. Had he managed to evade capture by the French? They had followed in the footsteps of the French reinforcements and had seen no sign of him, though it had been a nerve wracking journey for Camberwell, afraid at every turn that he would come across Will's dead body, left by the roadside as a grizzly reminder that the French were ahead of them. As it was, the boy's sudden departure had presented Richard Camberwell with a dilemma, for the last thing he wanted was for Will to be branded a deserter. Consequently, he had requested a meeting with Wellington himself before the news became general knowledge and had explained that Will had thought that by going ahead of the army, he could ascertain the whereabouts of the girls who had been kidnapped. Without actually saying so, he made it sound as though he had given the boy permission, and bore the angry length of Wellington's tongue for doing something so stupid. Fortunately for him, he had caught Wellington in a good mood, it being the day they were to start on the last leg of their journey to Badajoz, and the General had not proposed any discipline for either himself or for Will. It was also fortunate that Wellington seemed to have an unusually soft spot for Will since his exploits at Ciudad Rodrigo and was willing to overlook his unheralded departure as boyish recklessness. Camberwell thought he had managed to convince the General that Will had not deserted the army, but had just gone on ahead of it, assuring him that the army was Will's life, that he would never desert, and that if anyone could mingle unnoticed with the French in Badajoz, his servant would be the one to do it. However, he wasn't so sure when Wellington said sternly, "If you are lying to protect your servant, Captain, and I find out that he has deserted, then you will both be shot."

Camberwell shuddered as he left Wellington and hobbled back to his tent. He had conveyed his feelings on the subject with more outward confidence than he felt. He could only guess at the reason for Will's sudden departure. That he had gone in search of Megan was obvious, but why had he gone alone? Camberwell was worried, and again cursed Will's impulsiveness. Now he had three people to worry about. And Will had left Dodge to attend to his needs, his ankle still hurt, and it incapacitated him to a large extent, despite the crutches his men had made for him. He hated being anything other than robustly fit and he had clenched his fists around the wooden poles in frustration, irritated beyond measure as he hopped and staggered. All in all, it was a very angry man who had finally reached the tent, sank onto his cot, and shouted orders to poor Dodge who was doing his best to attend to his master's needs.

Now, at Badajoz, the tent was erected at last and Dodge proceeded to put Camberwell's few belongings inside out of the rain. Camberwell limped to the tent of a fellow officer whom he knew to always have a few bottles on hand and invited himself inside whereupon he partook of several glasses of wine that helped ease the pain of his ankle and put him temporarily in a better mood. By the time he went thankfully to bed that night on his narrow cot, with Captain Shaw already snoring on the other, Camberwell was drunk enough not to worry too much about Will, Sarah or Megan, and fell asleep to the rhythm of the rain.

He regretted his excesses the next morning and was not amused to be woken by a Corporal who asked that he meet with Wellington immediately. Wishing he had had time to eat, and looking less than immaculate, he waited for Dodge to saddle his spare horse, Dragoon, and then made his way through the rain to Elvas. He took George Trim with him to help, left him and the horses at a nearby inn, and limped his way into the house that Wellington had commandeered, using the crutches, cursing the clinging mud and the rain that still poured down.

"Ah, Camberwell," said Wellington as he entered the room where the General was eating a late breakfast. "Have you eaten?"

"No, sir," Camberwell replied, sitting down awkwardly on a spare chair.

Wellington immediately gave orders for one of his aides to provide food and, said nothing further as to the reason for the summons until he and Camberwell had finished eating.

Once the plates had been removed, the General sat back in his chair and frowned at Camberwell's appearance. "You look as though you had a bad night, Richard," he said.

Camberwell agreed that he had, though he felt better now that he had eaten. He was wondering why he had been called there.

Wellington came straight to the point. "We start constructing parallels tonight," he said, referring to the ditches that the British would dig to bring themselves and their guns closer to the walls. "But I could do with knowing what defences Badajoz has apart from the obvious. Is there any way we can get information from Will Tucker, Captain?"

Surprised, Camberwell stared at the General. "I doubt it sir. I don't know where Will is, or even if he made it into the city," he replied.

"He gave you no clue as to where he would be?"

"No, sir. He's never been inside Badajoz before." Camberwell wondered why Wellington would think that Will had. Wellington had besieged Badajoz unsuccessfully in the summer of the previous year but that was before Will had joined the army and while he himself was on sick leave in England. Then Camberwell remembered that he had given the impression that Will had permission to leave the camp. Wellington probably thought Will had specific instructions. The captain thought quickly and said, "Will's his own boss, sir. If he got into Badajoz, he'll be looking for the girls, but he'll also be taking great care not to be noticed. An Englishman in Badajoz right now will stand out like a wolf in a field of sheep."

Wellington frowned. "Damn!" he said, and was silent for a few minutes as though contemplating something. "Mark my words, Richard. This is not going to be an easy campaign," he said finally, then shook his head and pursed his lips. "Still, it has to be done. Yes, it has to be done."

"Yes, sir." Richard Camberwell wondered if the General was regretting the decision to come here. But there had been no decision to make. If the city was not won, then the war was lost.

"Go, Captain," said Wellington dismissing him with a wave of his hand, his irritation plain. "Damn girls letting themselves get kidnapped! We didn't need that on top of everything else. No, by God, we didn't!"

Camberwell saluted and left before the General could find something more to grumble about. Wellington hadn't even inquired about his ankle, he thought, but then he must have more important things on his mind than the consequences of an officer's carelessness.

He hobbled back to the inn where George had managed to persuade a pretty maid into giving him a bite to eat. Sitting by the window, George saw him coming. Stuffing the last piece of bread into his mouth and thanking the girl quickly, he ran outside to where Dragoon and the nag he had borrowed were tied to a bush. He helped Camberwell into the saddle, tied the crutches to his own and they left without a word being said, George curious to know what the meeting had been about but not daring to say anything as the captain's bad mood was very evident. They rode back to the British camp in silence. Once there, Camberwell limped to his tent, and shouted at Dodge to bring him some dry clothes. Then he spent the rest of the day brooding over Will's disappearance and what was to come.

*

The next morning Will awoke from a restless sleep while it was still dark. Opening his eyes he saw that the children were still asleep. When he moved, so did Scrapper who whined to be let out of the door. Will let him into the alley where the dog urinated prodigiously against the wall, then limped down the alley to forage for something to eat. Will's stomach also grumbled. The first thing to do was to find food, then he would look for the officer again. He was sure that if he could find and follow him, the Frenchman would lead him to Megan and the others. He called Scrapper softly and went back inside the room to find that Juan was awake. He beckoned for the boy to follow him outside, then told him they should go and look for food before the city was awake. The boy nodded, though there was a still a sullen air about him, as though he was resenting Will's interference. However, by the end of the first morning's foraging Juan was Will's devoted slave. He soon realised that here was someone well used to living off what he could gain by whatever means possible and they did well that morning, coming back to the room with a meaty mutton bone, a crushed loaf of bread, some half-rotted vegetables and ripe fruit, and half a skin of wine. Once Maria had made the meat and vegetables into a palatable stew, the children and Will fell on the food ravenously while Scrapper had a great time devouring the bone. The food and wine brightened the children's spirits. Afterwards Maria fetched water from a nearby well and thinned the left-overs into soup for the following day.

Will had explained to the children his reason for being in Badajoz and now Juan was very willing to help. He said he had been around when the reinforcements arrived and he had a good idea where they were billeted but he said the officers could be anywhere as they would take up residence in any house that could be vacated. He did, however, know the inns that were frequented by the French officers and he thought they would be a good place to start looking for the Major who was the only one Will had seen with Megan. The two of them spent the rest of the day haunting the inns but to no avail. They were not to know that Major Francois Deneuve was incapacitated that day with a hangover and upset stomach brought on by too much wine and brandy the night before. This caused him to stay in the house he had commandeered, at the same time causing much distress to Megan, Sarah, and Amy who had to put up with his negligence and presence, quite unable to decide which was worse.

*

The girls had spent an uncomfortable night squashed together on the merchant's double bed, hungry and worried. The room was cold as the fire had gone out and there was no more wood. Upon waking, Megan immediately tried the door but found it locked. This did not improve her mood and she even looked out of the window, trying to gauge whether escape would be possible that way. The room was on the first floor, with a balcony that ran the length of the house. A tree grew close by and she wondered whether they would be able to climb down it, but she could not reach any of the branches. She battered on the door, shouting that they needed food and water but no one responded, though many times throughout the morning they heard footsteps on the stairs and in the corridor outside their door. They were left alone until nearly noon when Deneuve, waking with a roaring hangover and only belatedly remembering the captives, opened the door without knocking. The room stank as the girls had been forced to use the chamber pot they had fortuitously found underneath the bed and the first thing an angry Megan demanded was that it be removed and washed out. The Major, grimacing at her loud voice, ignored her demands. Megan stamped her foot and also demanded that they be given food. Deneuve, unable to take her raucous shouting left the room without a word. More than an hour later a soldier came and gestured that Sarah accompany him with the chamber pot. Once it was emptied, she was escorted back to the room with a meagre meal for the three. The soldier also brought more wood for the fire which he lit. As he seemed a pleasant enough young man, Megan tried talking to him in the hope of enlisting his aid but his orders were not to converse with the girls, though he stared at them with a look Megan knew only too well. Eventually he left, and the girls spent boring, anxious hours alone until the evening when Deneuve, having spent the afternoon sleeping off his excesses, was in a better mood and brought in more palatable food which he intended to share with his captives.

The Major watched the girls eat and proceeded to tell them that he had been thinking over their plight. The British army had arrived, he said, and were presently setting up camp some distance to the east of the city. This fact stirred the hearts of the three captives, but they were not pleased to hear that Deneuve had it in mind to wait until the siege was over before telling a defeated Wellington that he could have the girls back in exchange for money.

"He will not do that," scoffed Megan.

"Maybe yes, maybe no," said Deneuve. "That depends how much he likes your husbands. Of course, if they are killed, then he will not want you back and we will keep you. And if your generals give up the fight and leave, we will send them a message to tell them we have you and expect to be paid for your safe return. Either way, you will have a long wait, ladies. It will take some long time – weeks probably – before your army is in any position to fight us. In fact, I doubt they ever will. Badajoz is very well defended and I do not think your puny army will ever take it."

Amy started to weep softly, Sarah looked dazed at his words which promised no hope of a quick release, but Megan was angry. She stood up, tipping the plate that was on her knee onto the floor.

"Your plan is preposterous, Major! I demand that you let us go this instant!" She ran for the door that had been left ajar, shouting for help, though where she thought that help would come from, even she had no idea. The Major was there before her. He caught hold of her and pushed his face close to hers, so that she reeled back from his stinking breath.

"You will behave, madam, otherwise it will be the worse for you," he said coldly. His brown eyes leered at her. "I have been very patient with you so far but that patience is wearing thin. You would not want to become my soldiers' plaything now, would you? That can easily happen, and if you are returned to your husband he will not want you because we will have made you a whore. I have seen the looks my men give you and your friends. They would like nothing better than to tumble you in bed, my lady, and it is I who act as your only protector. It would behove you well to remember that and to do as I say."

He let go of Megan's hands and pushed the door shut, then shoved her towards the bed. "Sit down and eat. Who knows when you may get the chance again." He gave a semblance of a smile. "With all my duties I may forget you are here." Having seen some evidence of this already, Megan angrily picked up her plate and sat down on the edge of the bed next to Sarah, but her thoughts were far from food. The news that the British army was outside the walls gave her renewed hope. If the army was here, then so was Will, and Will was resourceful. He would find a way into the city and rescue her. It was a hope she had to cling to for the alternative was despair and she would not resign herself to that. No. She would try and work out a plan of escape for herself and the other two, but if that proved impossible, she would cling to the thought of Will. He loved her and he would come, she was sure of it. Giving Major Deneuve a very black look, she took some meat from the platter in the basket he had brought, and started to eat.

Chapter 8

That night the air around the city of Badajoz was torn apart by the sound of French guns firing upon the British soldiers who dug away at the muddy ground with picks and shovels, making trenches which would get them and their own guns closer to the walls. As though to warn them that this was a futile exercise, the rain came down in torrents. The thunder banged in huge rolling waves of sound and the lightning flashed, making a difficult job even more harrowing. Mindful of their previous experiences of digging ditches under fire at Ciudad Rodrigo, the soldiers did their best to keep their heads down, but it was no good. Once the big guns shooting out of the embrasures in the city walls and bastions had their range, nothing could stop the gouts of earth and mud that flew up into the air, covering the digging men and filling in the trenches they dug. The noise was endless, searing the ear-drums, and the balls and shot found their mark, killing and wounding men.

"This is just the start, boys," shouted Sergeant Readman cheerfully to the young men manfully digging on either side of him, his voice at parade ground volume to compete with the French guns. The night was dark and very wet, the only light coming from the almost constant flashes of fire from the guns, and the lightning. "Whoa! Watch it there, Trim!" Reed yelled as a blast sent up a huge plume of earth near George Trim at the end of the line, covering the youngster with mud. He smiled at George who swore as he wiped the mud from his eyes, and slammed his spade into the pile of earth that filled the trench in front of him – earth that he had spent the best part of the past half an hour digging out.

The rain soon washed the rest of the mud from George's clothes but his feet stuck into the glutinous mixture and his boots were full of it. Muttering under his breath and shovelling again, he thought back to his carefree days as a clerk and wondered what on earth had possessed him to join up. He glanced sideways along the trench at his friends. Next to him, Bob Tomkins was keeping up a constant chatter as usual but appeared to be talking to no one. You couldn't hear anything above a shout anyway. George thought that Bob was probably talking to give himself courage. Beyond Bob was Nat Binns; short, ugly, a past thief, but a good man to have on your side in a fight. On the other side of Nat was Ron Parker, ex-blacksmith and the opposite of Binns, big, strong and, even now, hauling dirt out of the ground twice as fast as any of them. The sky lit up again and George ducked automatically as the whine of a shell passed overhead but it landed harmlessly in a dirt heap some way behind them. He shovelled out another spadeful of muck and thought about the friend who was missing. Will Tucker. Where was he? Was he still alive? Had he managed to get into the city before their arrival? At least he wasn't having to do this awful hard and dangerous work, but he would be in danger too if he was inside the walls. There were five thousand Frenchmen in Badajoz and rumour had it that Marshall Soult could be on the march soon with a helluva lot more. George looked up at the distant walls of Badajoz and thought that if they didn't get a move on, the army could be caught like rats in a trap – five thousand Frenchmen in front of them, and God knows how many more behind. The thought made him wipe the constant rain from his dirty face and quicken the pace of his digging. Will could look after himself. George just hoped that all this digging would do some good and enable the army to get closer to the walls so they could make a breach and get inside, then maybe he could find his friend. The thought cheered him up and he set to with his spade without any further mishap until the relief diggers came and he could thankfully retire to an exhausted sleep. He didn't even hear the guns that banged throughout the rest of the night.

*

The small family Will had befriended were sleeping soundly when the first guns rent the air with their horrible noise. Scrapper started to bark loudly and the two little girls immediately began to cry. Maria, white-faced, cuddled them both as Juan got up and lit a candle and Will carefully opened the door. Footsteps could be heard running along the street beyond the alley and he heard shouted orders as French soldiers marched past.

"What is it?" Maria asked as Will shut the door.

"The British must've started digging parallels – ditches," he answered. "The French're firin' at 'em. Yer'd best get used ter it. This'll go on for days."

The family didn't get much sleep that night, but Will still went out with Juan early in the morning, soon after a rainy dawn. Today he was determined to either find the officer who had Megan, or the French stores. He needed to get enough food to feed the family for a few days. He wanted to spend more time on the reason he was here, but he couldn't in all good conscience let the family starve. They were helping him by letting him stay with them so finding food was his way of payment. Besides, he had to eat himself.

He and Juan had a bit of luck that morning. They saw a mule train being herded through the streets and decided to follow it. The panniers on the backs of the animals were full and the man who was driving them was having a bit of trouble getting the lead mule to go in the right direction. He was a heavy-set man and threatening the poor animal with a stick, shouting, and causing it to bray loudly and skitter on the cobbles so that the panniers were in danger of slipping off its back. Watching from an archway that led into one of the plazas, Will had an idea. He spoke softly to Juan, who nodded. The boys went boldly up to the man, Juan in the lead. The youngster spoke to the man in quick Spanish, while Will kept his head down as much as possible and said not a word. The man stopped threatening the mule and slowly nodded. So it was that Will and Juan helped the man keep the mules heading in the right direction and discovered that the bulk of the French stores were being kept in the castle on the hill to the north of the city.

That it was guarded was obvious, and the mule train was stopped at a door set in a side wall which seemed to be the only way in. There were heavy gates in the walls but for some reason these were not opened and everything had to be taken from the mules' backs and into the castle through the small door. The mule herder was glad of the boys' help as the guard just leaned against the wall and seemed unprepared to do anything at all except stand and watch them struggle.

Hauling one of the heavy panniers between them, Will and Juan followed the trader into the castle. The pannier they were carrying was full of vegetables. Juan had conversed with the trader and found out that a lot of the stores of food that had been brought into the city before the siege were now being transferred into the castle for safe keeping. They were told to take the vegetables to a store-room where there were many more sacks like the ones in the pannier.

The boys helped the man all morning, fetching more food; meat, vegetables, flour, grain, wine, and fruit from various places around the city and taking it to the castle. Will was overjoyed. It was giving him a great opportunity to get to know the city, and to find his way about the castle. Who knew when he might need the information he was gathering all the time as they drove the mules from place to place? The boys took their chances too, and when they were alone, stole some food to take back to

Juan's family. This they hid behind rocks on the hillside upon which the castle stood, hoping that no one else would find it, but the incessant noise of the big guns still firing at the British soldiers gamely digging trenches was keeping most of the citizens inside their houses, and they saw very few people other than French soldiers all that day.

Will kept an eye open for the officer he needed to find and was finally rewarded near dusk when they went to a part of town they had not been to before and he saw the man coming out of an inn. He desperately wanted to follow him, but they had not finished their work yet. The muleteer shouted at the boys with some urgency. He wanted to be finished before the daylight faded completely, so Will took note of the inn and vowed he would keep watch there the next day in the hope of seeing the Frenchman again.

The trader in charge of the mule train was essentially a fair man and, at the end of a hard day's work, he rewarded the boys with a sack of food. "The French've just about got every mortal bit of food in the city," he said in Spanish to Juan. "But I'm not above keeping a bit back for my family and you boys've done a good day's work today. Old Conchita there." He pointed to the lead mule. "She can be a bit stubborn as you've seen and I appreciate the help." He stopped and listened as a gun roared from the city walls. "Looks like we're in for a spot of bother for a week or two, lads, so you just keep yourselves safe now."

Juan expressed their gratitude. The boys walked away to fetch their small hidden hoard, put it into the sack with the rest and went back to the room well pleased with themselves.

The next day Will went by himself to the inn where he had seen Deneuve and hung around until told to move off by an irate officer who threatened him with his horse whip. Will moved away but only to a convenient corner from where he could still keep the inn in view. It was not until the afternoon that he saw the man enter the inn with some friends. They were talking and laughing loudly. Will itched to get his hands on Deneuve. He was having nightmares thinking of what might be happening to Megan, Sarah, and Amy at the hands of this man and his colleagues and he had difficulty controlling his temper knowing he was but a few short yards away. But he would be stupid to show his hand at this stage. No. He must follow him, see where the girls were being held, and think of a plan to rescue them. Never did it occur to him that he might be unable to accomplish it. That was what he had come here to do, and do it he would.

Deneuve did not move from the inn until evening by which time Will was thoroughly bored, soaked through by the incessant rain, and hungry. Deneuve sent for his horse which had been stabled at the back and mounted with some difficulty, lower ranking officers, evidently eager to please, helping him into the saddle. They went as a group and Will, forcing stiff, wet limbs to move, followed at a safe distance. The officers led him to a large house only a few streets away, a house enclosed within a walled garden and Will felt a stab of excitement. Something told him that this was where the French were holding Megan, Amy and Sarah. He decided not to chance going through the guarded gates just yet but scouted round the outside of the walls, finally finding what he was looking for – a tree that overhung the wall. He climbed the slippery trunk and, hidden in the sparse foliage, looked over into the garden. From here he had a good view of the house and could see a groom taking two of the officers' horses to a building closer to him, a long stone shed he assumed was the stables. He saw that the house was two storeyed with a balcony running around the top floor. He wished he had a telescope to get a closer look. He clambered back down to the ground and leaned against the wall, thinking. First he had to get the girls out of the house, but then he would have a bigger problem – how to get them out of Badajoz. And once he had them out of the house – if he managed to do that at all – he would have the French after him too. He was tempted to sneak over the wall and see what he could do now, but knew this needed thinking about. The girls had already been captives for several days and if they were going to be raped it was probably already too late, though his mind baulked at the idea. Their rescue could wait another day and he wasn't even certain that this was where they were being held. He would go back to Juan's hovel, eat, sleep, and think it over.

He pondered the problem all the way back to the children's room. The rain had lessened to a drizzle and he had his mind fully on the problem, so it wasn't until he entered the alley that he became aware of shouts and a dog barking. Recognition dawned immediately and, with it, trepidation. Knowing Scrapper would get just as bored as he with waiting around the inn all day, he had left the dog with Maria but the sound he could hear was not Scrapper's happy, joyful barking. It was interspersed with growls and the shouts were desperate. What was going on? There was only one way to find out. Taking the knife out of the string belt that held up his trousers, Will ran to the door and kicked it open.

*

Lieutenant Pierre Bordeaux threw his jacket down on the bed in the room he shared with a fellow officer and picked up a decanter of port from the table by the window. He had been drinking with Deneuve and the others in the inn all afternoon but the wine did not seem to have allayed the restlessness he felt within himself. He poured a glass of the deep red wine and drank it down. The feeling had been with him ever since their arrival in Badajoz. It stayed with him even when on duty, patrolling the walls, making sure the gunnery sergeants were doing their job in trying to slow down the British trench digging. He hated siege warfare. The incessant noise of the big guns gave him a headache but it wasn't the guns that were making him restless now. It was the knowledge that the English girl was in a room along the corridor – a room he had been forbidden to go near by Major Deneuve who was the only officer allowed in. Bordeaux wondered if he had taken the girl already. Probably not. He had heard no screams from the room, only shouts and banging on the door. Deneuve was being a gentleman. For now. But Bordeaux wondered how long that would last. From what he knew of Deneuve and what he had seen in other towns, the officer was not above raping servant girls or taking women when he wanted them. There was one thing Deneuve liked better than women though, and that was money. The bastard probably wanted to ransom them. Yes. That would be just his style. Well, Bordeaux wasn't going to wait until the British possibly made a breach and the fight would begin in earnest. He wanted the girl with the curls and the beautiful face. And he wanted her now.

Swaying with drink, he closed the door to his room and made his way to the end of the corridor, to the room where the girls were imprisoned before realising that the door would be locked and he didn't have the key. He stood and thought for a moment. The officers who had drunk with him that afternoon were downstairs eating but with a skinful of wine in his belly he had not wanted food. His befuddled mind was still wondering how to get hold of the key when a soldier carrying a tray climbed the stairs halfway along the corridor and started to walk towards him.

Bordeaux realised that here was his chance. "I'll take that," he said to the soldier. "Give me the key." Before the puzzled man could do anything, Bordeaux had picked up the tray and was holding out a hand for the key. The soldier handed it over, shrugged his shoulders, and walked back towards the stairs. Bordeaux put the tray on the floor and fumbled the key in the lock then picked the tray up and pushed the door open with his foot.

Bordeaux saw that two of the girls sat on the bed, but the one he wanted was standing at the window. They were all staring at him, startled to see the man who had captured them, and not Deneuve whom they expected. They said nothing while he put the tray on the table, but the girl by the window frowned as he stumbled on the frayed rug.

"Eat," he said, waving a hand expansively at the tray. Sarah and Amy stood up and tentatively fetched some of the food but Megan had other ideas. She could see that the lieutenant was drunk and that he stared at her. Her quick brain told her that he had come to this room with ideas other than that of providing them with food and her mind raced as to how she could put his drunken state to her advantage. He started towards her, ignoring the other two girls and she pulled away from the window, eager to get between him and the door. Although trying to think how this situation could offer a way out, he scared her and her mind went back for a brief moment to Lieutenant Deaville. This French lieutenant had the same depraved and lecherous look in his eyes that the English officer had had when he'd pushed her down in a muddy field and climbed on top of her.

Bordeaux was speaking to her, telling her how beautiful she was and she stepped backwards but then was stopped by the edge of the bed. Sarah and Amy had stopped eating, realising that Bordeaux spelt trouble. Amy had her eyes closed, face hidden in her hands, as though wanting to detach herself from whatever was coming, while Sarah, made of sterner stuff, was looking desperately around for a weapon of some sort. Bordeaux reached out for Megan but her hand went up and she slapped him as she had before. Megan knew immediately that she had done the wrong thing. Bordeaux had been in the bemused, befuddled state of the quiet drunk. Now he was angry. He swore at her in French and reached for her arm again but Megan had run around the other side of the bed, also looking for something with which she could fend him off. Then she remembered Will and what he had done to stop Deaville from hurting the whore Juanita back in the village tavern at Christmas time, and she shouted, "Sarah! The chamber pot!" Sarah immediately knew what she meant and picked up the pot from where it lay just under the bed. Growling with anger, Bordeaux reached for Megan again but Sarah swung the chamberpot round and crashed it into the side of his head. Urine slopped out onto Bordeaux's skin, shirt, and uniform trousers. He swayed with a silly expression on his face for a second, before crumpling to the floor.

"Come on! Quickly!" Megan pulled a stunned Amy to her feet and the three girls ran out of the room, Megan only stopping to close the door behind them. They ran to the head of the stairs, only to see Major Deneuve standing at the bottom, talking to a fellow officer. They tip-toed along the corridor into a room at the end where the door was open. The room was small, scarcely more than a closet and, fortunately, empty. Megan closed the door and looked out of the window. There was a tree growing against the balcony and it gave her an idea.

"Open the window!" she hissed to Amy and Sarah. Sarah ran to push up the sash. She pushed as hard as she could but it wouldn't budge.

"It's stuck!" she said through gritted teeth.

Megan ran to help her and between them they strained at the wood. Suddenly the window shot up with a clatter. All the girls stood still and silent, expecting that someone must have heard the noise, but no one came.

"We're in our under clothes!" Amy wailed as Megan grabbed her hand and pulled her across to the window.

"Shh! Don't worry about that, you silly girl!" Megan whispered, angrily pushing Amy's head out into the rain. "Which would you rather do? Be raped by a Frenchman or be free in your undies? Now climb out of the window onto the balcony! Quickly, before they discover we've gone!"

It wasn't easy for the girls to step from the slippery balcony onto the nearest tree branch. There was a bit of a gap and Amy dithered for so long that Megan was sure their absence would be discovered before they could escape. "Come on, Amy!" she said in frustration as the girl whimpered and stretched her arm ineffectually for the sturdy branch. Eventually, Sarah said, "I'll go first." So they pulled Amy back, and Sarah clambered over the side of the balcony. "Hold my hand," she said to Megan and Megan held her as she reached out for the wet tree limb. She clutched it and managed to get a leg across to the fork before letting go of Megan's hand and grabbing the branch with both hands. Breathing hard, she and Megan then helped a very nervous Amy across and down to the next fork, before Sarah helped Megan herself. Once in the tree it was quite easy to climb down to the ground.

Darkness shrouded the girls as they crept through the garden shrubbery towards the wall at the back of the house, automatically avoiding the front gates, expecting, quite rightly, that they would be guarded. They saw no one, the French happily beside warm fires in the house and blissfully unaware that their prisoners had made their escape but Megan was thinking hard. Supposing they could escape the garden, where would they go? They were strangers in a city over-run by the enemy. She pushed negative thoughts to the back of her mind as they helped each other over the garden wall, at almost precisely the spot where Will had looked over only a short time before, but the problems came back when they found themselves in a dark street. Here they were, she thought, three English girls in a city full of French and Spanish, on the run and with two of them half-naked. She glanced at Sarah and Amy and saw they were staring at her, obviously as frightened as she, but looking to her for guidance. She mentally took control of her racing brain and tried to think clearly. First things first. The others needed clothes. And they all needed food. She thought of Will and what he would do in this situation. Steal. That's what he'd do. So that's what she would do as well.

She explained her plan in whispers to the others, refusing to listen to their nervous resistance. She set off down the street, keeping to the shadows, and there was nothing the other two shivering girls could do except follow her.

Chapter 9

The scene that met Will's eyes when he opened the door of the room the children lived in was one he had not expected. A boy and girl he did not know were huddled with Maria and the little girls near the mattresses, while a French soldier had Juan in a tight grip, attempting ineffectually to fend off Scrapper who was growling and trying to grab his leg. The man had a hand around Juan's mouth but the boy was struggling hard. Baby Carlotta was crying in Maria's arms while Rosa was staring with frightened eyes at Juan and the soldier.

Will approached the man warily, holding the knife in his right hand. "Let him go," he said in English. Startled at hearing the language, the soldier, dressed in the blue uniform of the French infantry, looked surprised but he kept a tight hold on the struggling Juan while still kicking out at Scrapper. Will thought briefly about throwing the knife but knew that if he did so he had a good chance of hitting Juan who would not keep still.

"Call off the dog!" said the Frenchman in accented English. "Or I will kill the boy." Will saw that there was a pistol in the hand that was not wrapped around Juan's face. To lessen the threat of the man actually firing it at Juan or one of the other children, Will reluctantly gave Scrapper a command and the dog, also reluctantly it seemed, backed away, though low growls still rumbled from his throat.

There was almost silence in the small room as the terrified children watched the soldier. He was tall and thin with a face that was all angles and his hair hung lank and greasy. The beginnings of a moustache graced his upper lip. Now that Scrapper was no threat, he appeared nonchalant, as though waiting for something. Before Will had even time to register this, two more soldiers burst through the door, muskets at the ready. The girls screamed and Will turned to defend himself but was too late to do anything about the musket butt that crashed down on his head. The knife fell from his hand and he dropped to the floor. The last thing he heard was Scrapper yelping in pain before everything went black.

*

"Will! Will! Wake up!" Someone was shaking him and there was a horrible smell. Will opened his eyes, but everything was foggy. The shaking continued. "Bugger off!" he said, flailing with his arms.

Whoever was doing the shaking let go and he sat up, his eyes gradually focusing until he saw Maria kneeling next to him and the other children gathered round, all staring at him with worried faces. The strange girl was holding the baby.

Will looked around. "Where are we?" he asked, then realised something was missing. "Where's Scrapper?" he asked in alarm.

"One of the men. 'e kick 'im 'ard and 'e not get up," said Maria with tears in her eyes. "They brought us 'ere. Juan and Antonio," she gestured to the other boy, "got caught stealing a musket from a sleeping guard. They ran and thought they 'ad got away but another soldier followed them, the one who was there now. 'E must 'ave called for 'elp on the way." The girl looked at Juan and started to cry. "They are going to 'ang them. And you because you are English."

Will felt an awful dread in the pit of his stomach but that was almost buried by the anger and grief he felt at the loss of Scrapper. He put his hand on the side of his head and felt a sticky mat of hair. Trying to put the thumping headache out of his mind, he attempted to concentrate on the situation. "Why did they bring the rest of yer?" he asked.

"They want us to watch the 'anging," said Maria in between sobs. She directed a flood of angry Spanish at her younger brother who sat with his friend, white-faced and near to tears himself. Will presumed she was angry with him for trying to steal the musket. Juan answered her and pointed to Antonio. Will looked at the other lad. He was bigger than Juan and had probably been the instigator. Will stood up, and wobbled as his head spun. He caught hold of the corner of a chest of drawers that stood next to him, and wondered why the French had not strung up the boys on the spot. Why had they been brought here? And where was here?

"Where are we?" he asked. He looked around the room, lit by two candles, noticed broken pottery on the floor and on a big bed that took up most of the room. He went to the window and looked out, then got a shock for he recognised the wall at the end of the garden below, and the street on the other side. Surely this was the house he had stared at from the tree by the wall only that afternoon – the one where he thought Megan was. Immediately his heart lifted but his optimism didn't last long for just then the door opened and a French captain entered the room.

"Take him," the officer said in French, pointing to Will, and made way for two French soldiers to come into the room. They grabbed Will roughly by the arms and marched him out of the door. He was taken to another room and pushed into a chair. The room had once been a store-room of sorts for there were shelves, now empty, but the chair was the only piece of furniture. Will began to struggle but the knock on the head had made him weak and he was no match for the two burly Frenchmen who tied his arms and legs to the chair and then left. A few moments later the door opened again and the Major he had followed that day entered the room. Will felt a wave of hatred wash over him. This was the man who was keeping Megan prisoner.

"You are English." The officer stared at him coldly. It was not a question so Will did not answer. His hair and eyes gave him away. He stared back at Deneuve who sighed and tapped a stick he carried against his thighs. "You would do well to co-operate," said Deneuve. "If you do, it may save your young friends from a hanging."

Not me though, thought Will. He said nothing. "My name is Major Deneuve. You can start by telling me your name." Deneuve still tapped the stick. Will decided there was no harm in telling him.

"Will Tucker," he said, giving no indication of his army rank.

Deneuve smiled, obviously pleased that his vague promise to release the other boys had had some effect. The two Spanish peasants meant nothing, but this English one intrigued him. "What are you doing here in Badajoz?" he asked.

Will didn't answer. What could he say? To tell the officer he was trying to rescue the girls Deneuve held prisoner would only lead to more trouble and indicate that he was a soldier. His negative attitude brought him a whack on the shins from the stick in Deneuve's hand. More silence brought him another one, this time on his shoulder.

"I think you are an English spy," said Deneuve conversationally. "Why else would you be here? I do not know how you got into the city, but I think the army sent you to spy on our fortifications. How are you sending information out of the city? How are those children involved? Answer me!" His face set into an ugly sneer as Will still kept silent and he raised the stick, hitting Will across the head twice. The blows stung and the room spun. Will's head lolled on his chest and he wondered how much punishment he could take before he passed out or told Deneuve the truth. Richard Camberwell had once told him that every man told the truth under torture eventually. However, Deneuve seemed to have another plan. "You keep silent now but you will tell me everything I want to know tomorrow," he said confidently.

"Tomorrow I will hang the two boys who tried to steal the musket. If you want to save your friends, you will talk." He untied the ropes that fastened Will to the chair and opened the door. The two men who had brought Will there stood guard outside. "Take him back," said Deneuve. His face twisted in a look of intense anger. "And make sure he doesn't escape like the others or it will be the worse for you. We will see tomorrow if a hanging loosens his tongue."

The older children were sitting despondently around the room when Will was pushed back into it. The two solders left them and locked the door. Maria exclaimed over the blood on Will's head and immediately tore a piece off her drab dress and spat on it, then tried to wash some of the blood away. Although her gentle ministrations hurt, Will let her do it, recognising that the girl was only trying to help. As she washed the cuts, he remembered what Deneuve had said. Something about others escaping. Could he possibly mean Megan, Sarah and Amy? If so, it was ironic that he who had come to rescue them had been taken prisoner instead.

His thoughts were diverted when the strange girl, pretty and petite, asked him where the soldiers had taken him. Her English was poor and Will, helped by Maria's translations over the more difficult words, took some time to explain what had happened, and who Deneuve was. He mentioned nothing about a possible hanging the next day, not wanting to upset the children. That he would have to think about later. The children settled into a depressed silence and Will took a good look at the girl. Seeing him watching her, she came and sat beside him on the floor. She said her name was Carmen Garcia and that she and her brother, Antonio, had lived on the streets for years. Their mother had been a whore who had died when Carmen was eleven and they had never known their father, or even if they had the same one. Looking at them, Will doubted it. Carmen's face was pretty dirty, but still attractive. She reminded him of a young Juanita, but the younger Antonio's nose was a different shape and his face was round whereas Carmen's was more oval. She seemed to like Will and stayed close to him.

Will saw that Maria, ever the little housewife, had cleared up the shards of pottery that had been strewn around the room. "They were from a chamber-pot," she said when he mentioned it. That explained the smell. It was old urine although he suspected that some of the foul odour came from Carlotta. The rags that Maria used for napkins had not been changed for some long time.

It was well into the night by now. Rosa and Carlotta had already fallen asleep, despite the ceaseless bangs from the French guns still trying to deter the British from their work in the trenches. One by one the others curled up on the big bed and fell into an exhausted slumber until Will was the only one awake. He lay on the rug before the dead fire, his aching head and the thoughts that whirled around in it, keeping him from sleep. He remembered again the Frenchman's words. Was it possible that Megan, Sarah and Amy had found a way out of this house, or had Deneuve been talking about other prisoners, maybe some Spanish nobles he had arrested, or even the people who owned the house?

It was very late when he heard a movement from the far side of the room and a shape passed in front of the window, silently coming towards him. As she got closer he recognised Carmen. The girl lay down beside him. "It is cold," she said, snuggling up to his side for warmth. Will said nothing but found himself glad of the company. Lately, despite being with the children, he had felt very alone. He thought of Megan. How was he to find her when he had all these children to get out of here? He felt somehow responsible for them and knew he must think of a way to prevent the two boys from being hanged the next day.

He was suddenly aware that a hand was stroking his leg. He looked over at the girl lying next to him. He could just about make out the whites of her open brown eyes watching him. "You are very – 'ow you say? – 'andsome?" she whispered. "I like to be with you. You like to be with me?" It took some seconds for her words to register, then Will realised what she wanted and he turned sharply towards her. "No," he said. "It wouldn't be right. Yer too young."

"I am seventeen," she whispered. The same age as himself. Good God! Her small build made her look about fourteen, but then Maria looked around twelve but had told him she was fifteen. "Do not worry," she said, her mouth by his ear. "I know men. How else must we eat?" Will was silent as he digested this information. This girl had probably kept herself and her brother alive by consorting with men from a very young age. Will's mind went back to Mary, the girl he had grown up with and with whom he had shared an on-and-off sexual relationship. No strings, just mutual sexual attraction and pleasure. He lay down again and before long the girl's hand was sliding up and down his trouser leg until it came to rest in his groin where things immediately started to happen.

It had been three months since Will had enjoyed two sexual encounters with Juanita. His relationship with Megan was chaste for several reasons, not the least of which was the eternal presence of her uncle and the fact that she was aristocracy, but it hadn't always been easy to refrain from the more physical aspects of loving her. Now here was this girl whom he did not even really know, offering herself to him and he was reacting as all red-blooded males would do in similar circumstances. What was he to do? He might be dead tomorrow.

In the end he didn't have a lot to say about the matter for the girl, taking his silence for acquiescence, pulled down his trousers, took off her own thin dress, and lay on top of him. Unable, and unwilling, to resist, he fondled her small breasts and stroked her thin body. She kissed him, and he responded, then she took him inside her and Will forgot everything for the next few minutes except the glorious feeling of desire and fulfillment that she gave him.

Afterwards he put his arm around her as she lay next to him. He felt a little guilty but also warm and tired. He kissed her on the cheek, and slept.

When he opened his eyes before dawn, Carmen was asleep on the bed with the girls. It was still dark but thoughts of what the day might have in store brought him to full wakefulness. He dragged on his clothes and stood up, then went to the window. They were on the first floor. He looked at the bed where the children slept amongst a tangle of sheets and blankets. Could he tie them together and climb down to the ground? It was worth a try. He wondered if he could get all the children to climb down. The boys and older girls would have no problems, but what about Carlotta and Rosa? He thought briefly about Megan. What if she and the other girls were still in the house? With difficulty he put her out of his mind. His first responsibility was to these children. He had to stop Deneuve from hanging the boys and that meant they had to get away somehow before the rest of the house woke up. He would think about how to find Megan later.

Will woke everyone up. The baby started to cry. She was hungry, as were they all, but Maria managed to quieten her. Will explained his plan and all the children were eager to comply. They opened the window with difficulty; the wet weather had warped the wooden frame and it took the three boys' combined efforts to shift it. The rain had stopped but the air was cold and damp. Will, Maria, and Carmen knotted the bed-clothes together. Will inspected the balcony railings but they were rusty and he was not sure they would hold, so he tied the last blanket to the iron bedstead. The younger boys went over the balcony and shinned easily down the rope first, glad to get out, then Maria with Carlotta tied to her back with a piece of blanket. Will went next, helping Rosa who was very scared, then Carmen last of all.

They might have got away without anyone knowing until much later except that the older ones' weight on the knotted bedding made the bed move towards the window and the noise of it dragging across the floor brought guards from the room below pounding up the stairs to see what was going on. Once all of them were on the ground, the children raced for the stable building and were hiding behind it by the time soldiers looked out of the window and realised they had gone. Peering round the corner of the stables into the half-light of an early dawn, Will saw two men leaning out of the window and hauling the bedding rope back inside. Then he heard shouting as the hue and cry went up and he pushed the others towards the wall. Juan and Antonio nimbly scrambled to the top of the wall. Will cupped his hands and heaved the girls up and the boys helped them over, then the little ones were lifted and handed down to the older girls. Last to go, Will heard a shot and a musket ball took a chunk out of the top of the wall. He hung by his hands and dropped down to the cobbles, then picked up Rosa. Maria carried Carlotta. "Run!" he told the children. They pelted down the street and didn't stop until they had put several streets and alleys between themselves and Deneuve's headquarters. At last, panting round a corner, Will called a halt. "Where can you stay?" he asked. All knew they could not go back to the hovel in the alley.

"They can come with us," said Carmen. "We 'ave a place near the cathedral."

"Go with 'em," Will said to Maria and Juan. He turned to go back the way they had come

"Where are you going?" Maria touched his arm, her expression one of concern.

"I 'ave ter go back. The girls I told yer about. I think they might be in that 'ouse."

Maria looked shocked. "You cannot go back. They will kill you!" she gasped.

"I 'ave ter," Will said gently. "Go. I'll find yer." He gave her a hug, did the same to Rosa, and to Carmen who gave him a knowing smile, then told the boys to lie low for a day or two and not to go anywhere near the part of the city they had just left. "I'll find yer," he promised, and set off back to the house.

Chapter 10

In the early hours of the morning, Amy and Sarah sheltered from the rain under the eaves of a house and watched anxiously as Megan entered another on the opposite side of the street. Wet through, they shivered and wished they had thought to bring some blankets off the bed to put around their shoulders. They had put as much distance as possible between themselves and the house that Major Deneuve occupied, keeping to the shadows, grateful for the darkness. Under the curfew that the French had imposed the only people they saw were French soldiers. It was easy to keep out of their way as they were mostly in large groups, either changing sentries, or relieving gun crews on the walls. French artillery still banged away, trying to stop the British from repairing the damage wrought during the day to the trenches and gun batteries.

The girls had kept away from the city walls where they were most likely to be discovered and were wondering where they could shelter for rest of the night when they had their first piece of luck. They saw a woman and a soldier, arm-in-arm, walking quickly down the street, their heads bowed against the persistent rain and not wanting to be spotted as the woman was breaking the curfew. The two entered a house that was adjoined to an apothecary's shop. Megan watched as closely as she could in the faint light from a nearby torch that spat and sizzled under the eaves of the shop and was pleased that there was neither sight nor sound of a key being turned in a lock, or of a bolt being shot. This gave her an idea that she explained to the other two.

"Megan! You can't, it's too dangerous!" Sarah hissed at her.

"I have to! It's the only way! You'll catch your death without any decent clothes." Sarah knew this was true. She and Amy hadn't stopped shivering since they left the house and, besides, it was so undignified to be running around in underclothes. She glanced once more at the house where a lamp had been lit, showing a comforting glow through the one window.

"All right then," she said. "But be careful!"

It was nearly an hour before the lamp went out – an hour during which the girls spent anxiously surveying the street for signs of possible pursuit, and becoming colder than ever. At last the house was in darkness again but Megan still waited for a full half hour before creeping across the cobbles.

Now, with the other two keeping an anxious lookout, as dawn was fast approaching, Megan turned the knob as quietly as she could, and opened the door. Inside, the house was pitch black. This would be more difficult than she imagined. She stood still for a moment and listened. A gentle snore came from a room to her right. She moved slowly and silently towards it, putting out her hands in case she bumped into anything but the passageway was clear. She entered a room and immediately her hands felt a bed-post. She sidled around the bed. The snores were louder here, and she could hear breathing too. Feeling her way around the side of the bed, she bumped into a chair and stood still, her heart beating so loudly she felt sure the occupants of the room would hear her, but they slept on. She felt around on the chair and her spirits rose when her hands touched material, lots of it. Quickly she bundled it up and crept back the way she had come, shutting the outer door softly behind her.

She ran back to the others who gave sighs of relief that she had not been caught. They hurried to where the flaming torch, protected from the rain by an overhanging eve, shed some light and they could examine Megan's findings. There was a dress and a cloak, the clothes the woman had been wearing when they had seen her coming down the street. The dress was big so Sarah took that and Amy bundled herself up in the cloak. Megan smiled at them both. Will would have been proud of her, she thought.

Clothed a little better, the girls then put their minds to hiding somewhere while they thought what to do next. They would have to keep out of the way of the French and there was no way out of the city. They needed some-where to lie low for a while.

They walked around the deserted streets in the rain until Sarah suddenly stopped and said, "I think we've been here before." She was right. Megan recognised the church they had just passed. "Damn!" she said. "We're going round in circles!" She leaned despondently against a wall. What were they to do? Where could they go?

"We'll just have to keep ..." she started to say when her ears caught the sound of marching feet close by. She grabbed Amy's arm and started to run, Sarah close on her heels. They splashed through the puddles down one street into another and around a corner then ...

Megan pulled up sharply and screamed. Pierre Bordeaux stood right in front of her, his face surprised, a look that was quickly replaced by anger and lust. His right eye was swollen and bruised where Sarah had hit him with the chamber pot. As shocked as he, Megan heard him snarl and felt him grab her arms before she could even think of running. Amy screamed and backed away while Sarah pulled at him, trying hard to make him let go of her friend. Bordeaux threw her off so that she fell, then he twisted Megan around so that she had her back to him. He put an arm around her throat, then took a pistol from under his coat and aimed it at the other two girls.

"Back off!" he said to Sarah. She stared at the gun in his hand. He would use it, she could see it in his face. Slowly, she stood up and stepped away from him. Amy felt for her hand and clutched it tightly. Megan screamed and struggled. "Be quiet, madam," Bordeaux hissed in her ear, "If you do not, I will kill your friends." They meant less than nothing to him. This was the one he wanted. He started to back away from Sarah and Amy, still keeping the pistol trained on them, then became aware of a sudden movement behind him. He turned his head to look. Too late he saw an arm come up and something hard hit the back of his head. He fell sideways to the ground, letting go of Megan who stumbled and nearly fell on top of him. Hands went out to stop her and she turned to see who it was.

"Will!" she breathed. She blinked, sure she was imagining things for Will looked very different from the soldier he had been, but it really was him picking up the pistol that lay on the ground near Bordeaux's hand and the rock that had stunned the Frenchman. Will straightened up and there was no mistaking that heart-melting grin she loved so much.

"Now what're three nice young ladies like you doin' in a bad place like this?" he asked, smiling through the rain while they stared at him in amazement. He bent to kiss Megan and she flung her arms around him. "Will! What are you doing here? How did you find us? What … ?"

"Watch out!" There was a sudden cry from Sarah, and Megan turned just in time to see Bordeaux rise up from the ground, a murderous look on his face, fingers fumbling for the pistol in Will's hand. She felt Will push her out of the way and watched in horrified silence as he struggled with Bordeaux. Then there was a loud bang. All three girls screamed, then there was silence for a few seconds before Bordeaux took a step backwards, his hands around a growing stain on his shirt-front. Will, the pistol loose in his hands watched in alarm as the officer slowly sank to his knees, then pitched forward onto the wet cobbles.

His heart thumping, Will hurriedly felt in Bordeaux's pockets for some ammunition. He found a small bag. "Come on!" he said and started to run, knowing that the shot would bring soldiers to investigate. Already they could hear shouts in the distance, probably the patrol they had heard a couple of streets away, Megan thought as she ran with Will. It was just their luck that there had been a lull in the gunfire from the walls at the moment when the pistol went off.

"Where are we going?" she panted as they ran from one wet street to the next. Will seemed to know, but she didn't have a clue. The streets all looked the same to her, and she had no idea where anything was in this city anyway.

"A safe 'ouse," Will replied, hoping he would be able to find the place near the cathedral that Carmen and Antonio called home. They ran until they could run no more, but when they stopped, out of breath, the only thing they could hear was the sound of the big guns firing, and there seemed to be no sign of pursuit.

Breathing hard, they walked until they came to the plaza. All was quiet. The cathedral brooded over the silent cobbles and pillars that provided a covered walkway on three sides of the square. Dawn was breaking though there was still heavy cloud and Will could only just make out the cathedral spires through the drizzle. Megan tightened her grip on his hand. He wondered where the children were. Carmen said she stayed near the cathedral. But where? Suddenly he saw a slight movement near a tall building on the other side of the square. A small figure moved away from deeper shadow for a second and Will thought he recognised Juan's outline. "There," he said, pointing. As he did so, there was a huge bang from one of the defender's guns and they ducked automatically, and when Will looked up it was to see a group of horsemen entering the plaza close to where he had seen Juan. Despite the rain, there was no mistaking the heavy figure on the lead horse. Deneuve. And there could be only one reason he was out in such miserable weather. The Major was looking for himself and Megan.

"Quickly!" he whispered and pushed the girls into the darkness afforded by the thick pillars. They crouched down. Will looked to where he had seen the small figure but it had gone. The horses had stopped and there seemed to be some discussion going on between the riders, then Deneuve walked his horse straight across the plaza towards the pillars that hid them. The girls huddled closer to Will. Will fumbled with the pistol, loading it quickly, ready to kill again if necessary. Deneuve stopped in the middle of the empty plaza, the rain falling steadily onto his tall fur busby. His eyes went all around the square. When his gaze reached their hiding place, Will and the girls held their breath. Nothing moved. Even Deneuve's horse stood like a statue. Then another gun banged and the horse shook its head, startled by the sudden sound. Deneuve seemed to stare right at them, then, thankfully, he looked away. Having surveyed the whole silent area, Deneuve turned the horse and walked back to his men. He pointed back the way they had come and in a few moments Will and the girls were the only people in the plaza.

Will led them around the walkway, keeping to the shadows until they came to the place where they had seen Juan. The boy made them all jump when he loomed up from the top of a flight of steps. He grinned at Will. "I was watching for you," he said and beckoned for them to follow him. They went down the steps and along a tunnel dank and dripping with slime, then through a broken doorway and into what had once been a cellar.

The room was lit with candles. The baby was asleep but the others were waiting for him anxiously. Maria said something in Spanish and crossed herself when she saw Will, smiling, pleased to see him, then she and the others stared at Megan and the other two girls. Silent little Rosa walked across to him and hugged him about the waist.

"She 'as missed you," said Maria "We are glad you find your friends."

Megan took her first look around the room. It was large, and furnished only with a few dirty blankets and wooden boxes that served as chairs and beds. Judging by the stink, an old bucket was their only toilet. There were shelves on the walls that contained an assortment of utensils and odd bits of clothing and a heap of rubbish stank in one corner. The whole place smelled of urine and damp.

"You must be 'ungry," said Maria. She could see Carmen staring at the newcomers and did not like the look on her face. Carmen and Will had thought her asleep when they had coupled during the night but she had heard Carmen's whisperings and knew what they were doing. It did not surprise her. Maria knew that Carmen prostituted herself for money and food, and Will Tucker was a handsome youth. But the girl who held his hand now must be the one he loved, and she could see why. Despite her wet, bedraggled look and torn, dirty dress, she was a beauty. Carmen was jealous and she, Maria, must diffuse the situation before Carmen said something and caused trouble.

It was a pity they had had to leave their store of food at the other house, thought Will, but even as his rumbling stomach reminded him that he hadn't eaten for ages, Maria was rummaging amongst the things on the shelves and produced some hard bread and apples which she shared amongst them. It was poor fare as the apples were soft and the bread hard, but filled their empty stomachs nevertheless. Later in the morning he would go back to the castle to try and steal some more of the French supplies, Will decided as he chewed a mouthful of bread. Juan and Antonio would have to stay here. It would be too dangerous for them to be about for a day or two. For him too, but someone had to feed these children. They had helped him. It was his responsibility to return the favour.

Thus it was that later that morning, Will made his way to the castle once more. He kept a wary eye out for Major Deneuve but he had spent some of the intervening hours trying to disguise himself. There had been a pile of clothing in the cellar; some stolen, other items those of Carmen and Antonio, but they had been only too pleased for Will to exchange his clothes that had been stolen in Ciudad Rodrigo for others. Now he wore a pair of ragged breeches and a dirty shirt, topped with an old coat that flapped about his knees. His bright hair was covered with a different coloured woollen cap. He hoped the disguise was sufficient to prevent Deneuve easily recognising him as he made his way to the castle. He missed Scrapper and wondered if his body was still lying in Maria's old house. Or maybe he was still alive somewhere. It was a thought he clung to. It had been good to have a dog and he felt the loss keenly.

The guns still battered the British who were spending up to sixteen hours a day digging trenches. Some of their guns were now able to return the French fire, though they were still too far away to do much good. Listening to the reports of the guns, Will felt a certain guilt, knowing that he should be there, digging with the rest of them, and he wondered what the senior officers' reactions were to his disappearance. Then he shrugged the thoughts away. There would be time to think about that later if he ever managed to escape the city. Now he needed to get food for the children.

He decided to wait near the castle in the hope of seeing the owner of the mule train again but though he waited for a couple of hours, he did not see him. No one was going in or out of the city now and he guessed that the stores in the castle would be well guarded. He would just have to brazen his way in. He searched about for something, anything, that would help him gain admittance to the castle, then his eyes lit on a pile of hay up against the wall nearest to him, and, close by, a small hand-cart that had obviously been used to transport it. Will looked around, but the sentries guarding the only entrance were round the corner, and there was no one on this side, though sentries patrolled the walls high above him. However, Will reckoned they would be looking outwards and not down into the streets below.

Quickly, he began to pile the hay back onto the cart, then he pushed it round to the other side where a bored sentry guarded the small door. The French soldier roused himself enough to bar the doorway and said something in French which Will took to mean that he wanted to know why he was there. Will played mute again, pointed to his mouth, then the cart and the castle. The man frowned, then his face cleared as he understood. He said something else and opened the door. Will pushed the cart through.

The door led into a short tunnel before opening out into a large clear space with open archways leading off it to rooms within. There were huge heaps of hay and fodder piled up against one wall so Will went and emptied his cart against one of them. The only Frenchmen he could see were walking or standing on the parapets of the castle. No one questioned his presence so he walked through one of the archways, trying to remember from his previous visit where the food was stored.

The archway led into a stone-walled room that was filled with sacks of grain. The room led to another so Will continued his search. This time he had better luck. Crates of fruit and vegetables were stacked on top of one another. Will went back to the other room and emptied a sack of grain behind some others, then took the sack and put some apples, root vegetables, and oranges inside. Carrying the sack Will searched other rooms, using Juan's knife to cut a slab of bacon from half a pig that hung from the rafters, lifting a small bag of flour and one of sugar from another room and then, best of all, finding a heap of dead chickens in a small annexe. By now his bag was full and he decided he had enough for a few days' meals. Carrying the heavy bag, Will walked out of the archway and back into the grassy place where the fodder was stored. Suddenly a voice rang out and he found himself accosted by an officer in the uniform of the Voltigeurs, the French equivalent of the British Light Infantry. He demanded to know what Will was doing there and things might have gone very badly for Will if the muleteer he and Juan had worked with before had not appeared at that moment in the doorway that led out of the castle. Seeing Will he smiled hugely and rushed across to greet him, then spoke quickly in Spanish to the officer. The Frenchman seemingly remembered the trader but was unable to understand the man's rapid speech. However, it appeared that the muleteer was indicating that Will had come with him. After several non-productive minutes of poor comprehension, the officer shrugged his shoulders and left.

The muleteer, thinking from their previous encounter that Will was dumb, put an arm about Will's shoulders and took him outside. Seeing the sack, he must have realised that Will was there to steal food, but, being Spanish, and not liking the French invaders, he ignored the fact. Without a word, Will managed to convey his thanks, only wishing he had been able to steal the handcart. It would have been good for his disguise to have been able to push it around the city, giving the impression he was on some errand but he did not dare speak for fear of giving himself away. The muleteer had other perishables on the back of his mules, given unwillingly by those Spanish people still in the city, and he gave Will another sackful, for which Will was very grateful. Now the children had enough food to feed them for a couple of weeks.

Will walked happily back through the streets, still watching warily for French officers, but he reached the cellar without difficulty, and the children were amazed at his good fortune. Sitting next to Megan, eating an orange, Will began to think about escaping the city. He needed to get to the British lines so that he could join in the fight. Listening to the incessant noise of the big guns, it embarrassed and annoyed him that he was not part of the force that was even now digging its way forward towards the city walls. He knew very well that it was hard and dangerous work, but his friends were out there and he wanted to be with them. He had accomplished what he had set out to do and now he must get out of the city.

It was a matter of pride.

Chapter 11

That night the children ate well. The cellar they were in led into a maze of such rooms and in one of them the boys laid a fire so they could cook a chicken. There was a small grated air vent at street level for the smoke to escape from and though Will was worried that the folk outside would wonder where the cooking smell was coming from, no one bothered them.

Now that Megan, Sarah and Amy were safely away from the French and the children had enough food to last for a while, Will grew bored and restless. The noise of the guns reminded him constantly that he should be outside the walls with the besieging army and he wanted to look for ways to escape the city. He prowled the streets, mostly alone, sometimes with Juan, but although he went pretty close to the city gates, he could not find a way out. They were very heavily guarded, and there was always the constant fear of being spotted by Deneuve as French soldiers and officers were forever patrolling. During these days, Will furthered his knowledge of the city until he knew his way around almost as well as the natives. He found other poorly guarded stores of gunpowder, weapons, food, and fodder, and these stores gave him an idea, one that he put to Juan one night when everyone else was sleeping. The boy was all for it and they woke Antonio to tell him of it. Will decided that if he could not help the British outside the city, then he would do all he could to make life difficult for the French inside it.

So began a time of torment for the French. Each night the boys slipped out of the cellar and made their way to one of the stores, or to stables or houses where the French were living. There they perpetrated all sorts of sabotage. They stole, spoilt, or destroyed ammunition, food, fodder, gunpowder, wine, carriages, and anything else that the French were using. Sometimes it was merely a case of stealing a case of musket cartridges, taking it back to the cellar, and getting the girls to empty all the gunpowder out of them so that they would not fire, or throwing a crate of cabbages into a midden, not without taking a couple for their own use first. They found that the small stores were easy to steal from at first, but after a couple of nights of harassment, the French doubled the guards and they had to think of other ways in which to sabotage the French effort. They took to hanging around outside the houses where the French officers stayed, or the inns in which they passed their off duty hours, and then the boys would steal the officers' horses and let them go in other parts of the city. The only place they did not go to was the castle. Will decided he had tried his luck once too often there already and it was now too well guarded, though it irked him that he could not get to the great stockpiles of weapons, food, and gunpowder there.

The boys had only been perpetrating their sabotage for a few nights when something happened to take the French officers' minds off their problems in the city for a while, and onto more serious matters. The rain stopped and the British attacked the Picurina fort to the south-east of the city. Hundreds of men, all volunteers from the 3rd and Light Divisions who were glad to be doing some fighting at last, hid in the trenches, then ran towards the glacis and the walls of the fort. Up the scaling ladders they went, and although they lost many men to the French defenders, the fort was taken, enabling the batteries of guns built into the trenches to pound away at the south-east corner of the city wall. This was the part that the British engineers deemed the weakest and where Wellington wanted to make a breach.

Now the noise became mind-blowing. The British siege guns battered the ancient walls while the French fired back, trying to destroy the batteries of guns built into the trenches. The British soldiers who had taken the Picurina fired the French army's own guns at the city's defenders. Sometimes the guns overshot, and houses near to the walls were hit, causing panic amongst the residents. This played right into Will's hands, for now the French were far too busy defending the city to worry too much about guarding stores. It became easy for the boys to steal and destroy and sometimes they risked day time raids as well. They found wineskins in a room behind the inn that was frequented by Major Deneuve and his men, and spent a happy few minutes with knives, flooding the floor of the room with wine that ran like blood. Will wished there was something more personal he could do to Deneuve, but the Major kept his residence extremely well guarded since Will's and Megan's escape and there was nothing Will could do there, though he vowed he would get his revenge when the British entered the city.

Megan sometimes persuaded Will to take her with him on his nightly prowls, though not often. They had many an argument over it, Will not wanting to risk her being seen by Deneuve and thinking, secretly, that he did not want to have to worry about her when he was trying to work undercover himself. However, Megan, as usual, refused to be told what to do, and she usually got her way. The tale she told of sneaking into the house to steal clothes for Amy and Sarah went a long way to convincing Will that she might not be such a hindrance, and a couple of times he gave in. Swapping clothes with Carmen so that she was dressed in ragged skirt and blouse, and with a hat to cover her curls, she became nearly as adept as Will at gliding through the dark like a wraith and was certainly a help in destroying French equipment and supplies which she did with great enthusiasm.

Carmen may have given Megan her clothes in exchange for Megan's once good dress, but that is where co-operation between the two ended. Carmen did not like the other girl at all and it soon became obvious to the others. When they were all together in the cellar, Carmen would give Megan surly looks and mutter in Spanish to herself. Maria was the only one aware of the reason. Thinking her merely unsociable, Megan ignored the girl but even Will, who had not been around as much to notice the animosity, spoke up when she deliberately threw a plate of food onto Megan's lap one evening, making the food spill onto her skirt.

Megan stood up and hurled abuse and the plate back at the girl who spat quick Spanish in return. Will looked on, bemused by the vitriol, but then he had to intervene quickly when it looked like the war of words was going to become physical. He spoke sharply to the two who, glaring hatred at each other, gradually settled down to eat. Later, before he, Juan and Megan went out, he took Maria to one side and asked her if she knew why Carmen did not like Megan. At first Maria did not know what to say, but then she told the truth.

"She is jealous," she said simply.

Will frowned. "Jealous? Of what?"

Maria gave a deep sigh, not wanting to give away the fact that she knew of his liaison with Carmen back at Deneuve's house. "Megan is yours. Carmen wants to be," she said diplomatically.

"Oh." Will was surprised, then thoughtful. Since Megan's arrival he had nearly forgotten the night of their capture and his coupling with Carmen in front of the dead fire. Had it actually meant something to her? He had thought she had merely wanted comfort and, as a girl who had many men, she would think nothing of the encounter except as a few minutes' pleasure. He ran his fingers through his dirty hair, then grinned. "Oh, well," he said. "Can't be 'elped. She must understand that I love Megan and no one's goin' ter come between us."

"It may not be that easy," warned Maria. "Carmen … she 'as a temper. She can be dangerous."

Will laughed off Maria's remarks but the next day he wished he had taken more heed for he was to find out just how dangerous Carmen could be.

Chapter 12

During the day, while the armies' heavy artillery banged away at each other, Will, Juan, Antonio and Megan tried to grab some sleep. They had got somewhat used to the noise of the guns but the days brought other sounds; horses, the shouts of officers, sometimes screams, dogs barking, carts rumbling, the sounds of a city under siege. However, the four managed at least a few hours' rest while Maria took the baby and Rosa in search of water or firewood. Carmen usually left early in the morning though where she went to, no one knew. She never said, and no one questioned her, though she sometimes returned with coins in her pockets and Will suspected she was meeting with French soldiers.

The French came to the cellar just before noon a few days after the British had started to bombard the corner of the city wall. The three boys were asleep, as was Megan. Late the night before they had stolen some muskets, powder, and cartridges from under the noses of two guards they had seen sleeping outside the French garrison headquarters and Will had spent some time that morning teaching Maria, Juan and Antonio how to load them. Now the weapons stood in a corner of the cellar.

Rosa had been left to look after the baby while Maria went for water. Carlotta was fretful and Maria was worried that she was getting sick so had not wanted her to go out into the damp, cold air. It was some distance to the nearest well and Rosa knew Maria would be a while, so she decided to amuse her sister with a ball of paper tied with string that she held while the baby lay on a pile of clothing and batted it with her small fists, gurgling with pleasure at the simple game. Amy and Sarah were in the cellar where the cooking fire was, busily preparing vegetables for a stew.

Suddenly the sound of heavy footsteps echoed outside the cellar entrance. Rosa looked up, startled to see a French soldier filling the doorway. He held a musket in his hand and was quickly followed by several more men, and an officer – Major Deneuve. Rosa let go of the paper ball and ran to Will who had woken at the noise and was scrambling to his feet, but the officer got there first. He pushed her roughly out of the way, then shouted that his men restrain the boys and Megan before they could escape. Rosa crawled back to her baby sister who was crying at the sudden disturbance, and held her tightly, then her eyes widened because Carmen had followed the men into the dimly lit room and was standing in the shadows.

Will, shocked, and yanked to a standing position by strong arms, struggled and protested loudly as Megan and the two younger boys were also roughly pulled to their feet and had their arms tied. Megan screamed and kicked at Major Deneuve who just smiled at her. He still smiled as he slapped her hard across the cheek.

"So we meet again, *mademoiselle*," he said in English, ignoring the look of hate that she gave him through eyes that glistened with tears. "And I see you have some friends that I have been looking for too." He looked at Will who glared back. "I believe you are behind the sabotage that has been going on this past few nights – you and these thieves. It seems I guessed right." He gestured towards the muskets. "You are a British spy." His eyes flickered over Juan and Antonio who looked scared to death. The eyes hardened and the smile was replaced by a thin line. "I also hear you killed one of my lieutenants. We found his body. At first I was under the impression that he had got into an argument with someone. Bordeaux always did have a hot temper. Someone saw you and it appears that you killed him while rescuing your lady who, it seems, is not married to an officer after all, and is probably not an aristocrat either. Well, you won't escape my clutches again. Neither will you," he said to Megan.

"You have no proof," said Will. He felt as though he was in the middle of a bad dream. Deneuve had captured him once. How could it be happening again?

"I have all the proof I need." Deneuve smiled again. "It would appear that you have … how you say … a traitor in your camp. Show yourself, *ma cherie*!"

Will, Megan, and the others all stared as Carmen stepped forward. In the few minutes it had taken for them to be overpowered, no one except Rosa had noticed her standing in the shadows behind some of the soldiers who barred the doorway and their escape. Will went white, and his heart fell when he saw the smile of utter satisfaction on her pretty face. She glanced his way and the look was one of revenge being very sweet. Now Will knew how Deneuve had found their hiding place and it was all his fault. If he hadn't treated Carmen so lightly, been so damn well eager to bed her, she might not have felt the need to betray them. Jealousy had been her motive.

"Bitch!" shouted Megan. "What have we ever done to you?" Will went even paler as he watched Megan struggling to get at the girl. How could he tell her that it was he who had brought this upon them? Rescuing the girls,

befriending Maria's family, sabotaging the French stores. It was all for
nothing. Now they were in an even worse mess than ever.

Deneuve slapped Megan again, and Will felt the rage well up within him.
The feeling gave him strength. They were not finished yet and he was not
willing to give up. He would find a way out of this mess. He would. He
growled, and struggled to get away, but Deneuve just laughed at his
ineffectual efforts.

"Now where are the other two ladies, I wonder?" he said, suddenly
realising that Amy and Sarah were not there. "Search the cellars!" The order
was snapped at the two soldiers not holding the boys. They went
immediately through the doorway into the next cellar but they came back a
few minutes later empty-handed.

"Well?" Deneuve demanded.

"There is no one, *m'sieur*," said one, shrugging.

"Where are they?" Deneueve tightened his grip on Megan's arms.

"They went out. For fire-wood," Megan invented quickly. Her cheek
smarted from the two slaps but she was not going to give up her friends
easily. She did not know where the girls were as she had been sleeping, but
knew they must be in the cellars somewhere. They had not been outside for
days, not since arriving at the cellar, for fear of being seen by the very man
who now held her.

Deneuve stared at her, wondering whether or not she was telling the truth.
Then he shrugged as if it did not matter. "Take them to the house," he said
to his men who restrained the three boys. "They will be hanged tomorrow
at dawn."

"What about them?" One of the soldiers pointed to Rosa and the baby,
cowering on the pile of ragged clothes.

"Leave them." Deneuve was not interested in small girls and babies. If
they starved, so what? His job here was done.

Within minutes they had gone. Rosa, frozen into immobility, sat on the
rags, her small face rigid with fear. Then, suddenly, she was being enfolded
in tender arms as Sarah knelt down beside her. "Are you all right? Oh, Rosa!
What a dreadful thing!" She looked at Amy who stared back at her.

"What are we going to do?" Amy whispered.

Sarah said nothing, but rocked the two children in her arms. Thoughts
were rushing through her brain like a river in flood. What to do? She had
heard the voices and Megan's screams and had rushed to peer in the
doorway of the cellar where they all lived, seen Deneuve and his men, then

tip-toed back to Amy and pushed her through a hole in the wall and into the blackness of the next cellar. There they had stayed, hardly daring to breathe while the two soldiers conducted their perfunctory search of the cellar containing the cooking fire. Fortunately the soldiers had looked no further, unwilling to go into the maze of dark cellars that ran under the plaza buildings. Once the two soldiers had gone back to Deneuve, Sarah had crept back and had heard everything. Now she wondered what on earth they could do to help.

Her thoughts were interrupted by the return of Maria, carrying a heavy bucket of water. The looks on the girls' faces told a story, and she dropped the bucket, spilling the water, her own face paling as she demanded to know what had happened. Her hand went to her mouth as Sarah told the tale and her eyes glistened with tears.

To give Amy, who was near to hysterics, something to do, Sarah told her to get them some of the wine that Will had stolen and was now hidden in the furthest cellar. They all needed fortifying. Her thoughts were settling now. Looking around the room, her gaze lit on the muskets that had been stolen the night before. So pleased had he been with capturing the boys and Megan, Deneuve had forgotten about them. The sight of the guns gave Sarah a surge of hope. They had weapons. Both she and Amy could use a musket. Captain Camberwell had insisted that the women who followed the men in his Company be taught at least how to load and fire one. They had muskets, ammunition, and a bag of gunpowder that had been stolen on one of the nightly forays. Her mind raced again. What to do? Then her eyes lit up. They had to find out where the boys were and cause a diversion. Something to distract the soldiers. But could Amy and Maria be relied on to help her? Amy was timid, and Maria only fifteen. Cautiously, she put forward her plan, unformed though it was. The other girls surprised her. Whether or not it was the wine that gave them courage, or their circumstances that had hardened them, she did not know, but they were quite willing to help.

"We'll make bombs," said Sarah, warming to the idea herself. "There are empty bottles in the next cellar." She picked up the paper ball that the baby had been playing with. "And we have string. We can fill the bottles with gunpowder and use the string as a wick."

"How will we light them?" asked Maria, following her train of thought. She was cuddling Rosa who still sat as though in a trance. The baby, in her innocence, had fallen asleep.

"Will's tinder box," Sarah answered. He always left it on a shelf in the cellar so they could use it to light the cooking fire.

"Do you think they've taken them back to the house we were in?" asked Amy. "Should we go there, do you think? It was dark when we left there, and we went down so many streets, I'm sure I could never find it again."

"I know where it is," said Maria. "Will told me the district and I recognise the house from his description." She lowered her head sadly. "It is close to where I live when Mama and Papa were alive."

"Good," said Sarah. "But we may not have to go there. We have to find out where the ..." She swallowed, then carried on bravely, " ... hanging is to take place. Amy, you get the bottles and we'll start to fill them."

As Sarah dragged the bag of gunpowder from its hiding place, Maria touched her arm. "Will it work?" she asked anxiously. "We are three women. There will be soldiers. And lots of people watching ..." She paused for a moment, letting the sentence trail, trying hard to swallow the lump in her own throat that threatened tears.

"We can't stand by and do nothing," said Sarah grimly, pushing away the doubts that surged up when she thought of the magnitude of their task. "Will and Megan are my friends. Juan and Antonio too. It has to work. It has to."

*

Will stared out of the window at the garden below and remembered when he and the children had escaped from this room only a few days before. Now the sheets and blankets they had used were gone and the iron bedstead was bare. There was nothing in the room that could possibly be used as a means to escape. Every stick of furniture except the bed had been removed. The room was cold, the fire out. Juan and Antonio sat on the floor, dejected and silent. Will was trying hard to come to terms with the situation, with no success. That he was the one who had brought it about lay heavily on his conscience, not so much for himself, but for the boys and Megan. And where was Megan? She had been taken away by Deneuve. What if, even now, he was raping her? He shivered at the thought, and smacked the wall with his fist, angry with himself. The two boys looked up, startled at the noise, but said nothing. There was nothing to say.

*

Standing on a worn carpet, Megan stared at Major Deneuve as he sat in his chair by the roaring fire of the house's drawing room and contemplated her.

Inside she was worried, and scared, but she tried not to show it. Why had Carmen done this to them? And what was Deneuve going to do with her? So far, apart from slapping her twice back at the cellar, he had kept his hands off her, but she suspected it would not last. She had seen that look in men's eyes before. The look of lust. This man wanted her, but did he want money more? Was he still thinking of exchanging her for money, or had he abandoned that plan? She waited for him to speak.

At last he did. "You do not like me." The statement surprised her. It was not what she had been expecting.

"*Non*," she shook her head. What else could she say? The man was at least fifteen years older than her, big, tough, and a Frenchman. Of course she didn't like him.

"You love the English boy?"

"*Oui*."

"He is very lucky. But he is not an officer. You lied to me."

Megan said nothing.

"You are not of noble birth?"

"I am." Megan drew herself to her full height and said with as much dignity as she could muster, "I am Lady Megan Camberwell. My uncle and grandmother own Camberwell Hall in Kent. It has been in my family for generations. My uncle is Captain Richard Camberwell of the 4th Kent Light Infantry."

Deneuve nodded. He believed her. Despite his question she had the look of an aristocrat. "And the boy? Who is he?"

"Will Tucker. He is my uncle's servant and a soldier in his Company."

Deneuve thought this very amusing. "You are in love with a servant? Does your uncle know?" he said, chuckling.

"*Oui*. We have his blessing." Megan thought of Will and what was to happen to him, and her demeanour crumpled like a wilting flower. "Please don't hang him. I'll do anything you want, but please don't kill him."

"Anything?" Deneuve's eyes lit up.

Megan realised suddenly what she had said, but she took a deep breath. For Will she would do anything. "*Oui*." Deneuve could hardly hear the word and knew what an effort it had taken for her to say it. For a while he just stared at her. Lieutenant Bordeaux had wanted this girl badly but Bordeaux had been a boor who couldn't keep his trousers buttoned. And now he was dead, and out of the picture. Deneuve knew that he could take this girl at any time, with or without her consent, but sometimes the anticipation was as good as the spoils. He twirled one end of his black moustache with his finger. He had never yet had to resort to rape. Women back in France, and in Portugal, had been very willing to consort with him. Besides, he had that girl, Carmen, the girl who had wanted revenge on *Mademoiselle* Camberwell and her beau for some reason. She would go to bed with anyone for a few coins. This girl excited him, he could not deny it, but he would enjoy the experience a lot more if she was at least half willing. Was she a virgin? He suspected it. She might be in love with a lad but he was willing to bet all the money in his purse that she had not yet been laid.

"I will remember you said that," he said. "The hanging will take place as planned. Tomorrow you will watch and you will see what happens to people who fight against us, then you and I will talk again."

"But you can't hang them! They're just boys!" Megan pleaded. "*S'il vous plaît*! Please! I meant it. I will do anything." She stood still for a moment, sighed, then slowly began to unhook the buttons of her dress. Her eyes never left his as he watched, mesmerised. Shaking inside, Megan tried not to think about what she was doing, but forced a picture of Will into her head. She would do it for him. She would let this man have his way with her if it would keep Will from the gallows.

Deneuve blinked and then stood up. He walked towards her, and Megan had to grit her teeth to stop herself from stepping backwards, away from him. He stood close to her, and she could smell tobacco and wine on his breath. He put a hairy hand inside her dress on one of her breasts, squeezing it uncomfortably. Megan gasped and had to force herself not to pull away. "Unfortunately, *mademoiselle*, whatever you do will not help your friend," said Deneuve in a low, tight voice. "If I stop the hanging, the Colonel of my regiment will want to know why, and I will be in grave trouble. If it was just the sabotage, there may have been a chance, but because he killed Lieutenant Bordeaux the boy must die. That is French law. There is nothing I can do. But …" He smiled and stroked her face, his pudgy fingers hot and sweaty. Megan flinched. "Tomorrow. That is another day. You and I will get to know one another better and we will discuss whether or not this uncle of yours will pay to have you back as a virgin, or whether I should assume he will be killed in the attack and seek payment from you."

Leaving Megan staring at the fire, he left the room. Megan gave a dry sob and sank to her knees, then let the tears flow, knowing there was nothing, she, nor anyone else, could do to help Will. Tomorrow he would die.

*

The gallows had been set up in the plaza not far from the cathedral steps. Maria had put herself in danger the previous evening by walking the streets seeking information as to where the hanging would take place. She had eventually found out from a drunken soldier who had reeled out of an inn and pawed her even as she questioned him. Feeling his hands tighten around her waist, she had wrenched herself free once she had the answer she wanted, and sped away, thanking God that the man was too drunk to follow her.

That the hanging was to be near the cellar was a piece of very good fortune for the girls as it resolved the difficulty they would have in transporting their home-made bombs through hostile streets. However, waking up to the sound of hammering the next morning as men erected the gallows made them realise just what they were undertaking, and Amy was all for backing out.

Sarah, anxious to the point of anger, shook the other girl hard when she voiced her misgivings. "We are going to do this, Amy!" she said, her voice strong and forceful. "Will rescued us from that Frenchman! He risked his life to come into Badajoz to rescue us! And the other two are just boys! We must do what we can to help them!"

The shaking stopped and Amy, her fair hair hanging in lank strands around her face, stared at her friend in astonishment. This was not the Sarah Harvey she knew, the quiet, polite girl who was usually so caring and thoughtful. This was a harridan, someone more like Megan Camberwell with whom she had never really got on. "But, Sarah …" she started.

"But Sarah nothing," said Sarah shortly, her hands still pressing Amy's to her sides and her face close to hers. "We have to do this, Amy, and I need your help. Don't start getting scared on me now. I need you to follow the plan we made last night. There's no backing out. You must do it! Do you understand?"

Slowly Amy nodded but as Sarah let go of her hands and went to Maria who was feeding the baby some mushed up bread and gravy from last night's stew, she wondered if she could go through with it. Sarah's plan was dangerous, as it had to be. Amy knew she was not like Megan Camberwell, or even Sarah. She hated excitement and danger, though there had been plenty of both since she had come to the Peninsula. She thought back to her childhood in the pretty cottage in Hampshire and the day she had met Corporal Seth Good, walking down the lane from his father's farm, on leave and all set to go off to war again in a few days. He had courted her for a week, seven marvellous days when she had fallen in love, and listened to the tales he told of glories in another country. He had asked her to marry him and they had gone to the preacher the day before he embarked at Portsmouth. Then Seth had used his silver tongue to persuade the Colonel of the regiment that she should travel with him. She had been pregnant within a month, but had lost the baby on the hard journey across Portugal, then poor Seth had been killed in a skirmish. Sergeant Rogers had been only too willing to take up with her and she supposed he was a good man, in his way, though he was very rough in bed and wanted her far too often for her liking. Now, here she was, pregnant again, and surely all the horrible things that had happened in the last few weeks would make her miscarry again, though there was no sign of it so far. She put a hand on her stomach and felt the small bump that was her baby. How could Sarah even ask her to help when she was in such a delicate state? Of course she felt sorry for Will, Megan, and the two boys, but really, was there anything they could do to stop the hanging? Would Sarah's plan really work?

She was brought out of her reverie by Sarah asking her to fetch the muskets and ammunition. As she lifted up the guns from their resting place in the corner of the cellar, she knew that however much she did not want to join in, she would have to do what Sarah wanted. She relied on her too much. Without Sarah, and Megan when she was around, she would probably be dead, or a Frenchman's moll by now. Sighing, she started to load the muskets.

Chapter 13

The next morning, Maria watched from the cellar steps with her hand over her mouth as Will, Antonio, and her brother were brought into the plaza under an escort of French cavalry. They stood in a cart pulled by a slow mule, a cart that rocked from side to side and threatened to dislodge their precarious footing. Tears ran down Maria's cheeks, but she bravely choked them back as she ran down the steps and into the cellar.

"They are coming!" she said. Sarah looked at her for a long minute, then at Amy, and nodded, then all three girls ran to their allotted tasks.

*

A large crowd had gathered. A few booed and threw sticks and stones at the three boys as the cart pulled up beside the wooden gallows that drew everyone's eyes in the plaza, but many watched silently, especially the women. Will, his hands tied behind his back, stared up at the gallows, bleakly. He heard a grunt and turned to look at Juan. Blood trickled down the boy's cheek where a stone had nicked it. The youngster was crying but Antonio's pale face was expressionless. Will looked at the crowd, women and children mostly, drawn by the spectacle as they would have been in London. He himself had seen hangings there, some macabre thread pulling him towards Tyburn to see the dying throes of criminals yanked on the end of a rope. Now here he was, about to have his neck stretched as they had had theirs.

The cart stopped with a jerk that nearly toppled the boys, and the few hecklers in the crowd fell silent. Now the only sounds in the plaza were the British and French guns that still periodically battered away at each other. But in this small space they seemed to be in another world as the scene in the plaza unfolded. The people watching showed little pleasure at being there. Most were Spaniards, unwilling to support the deaths of two of their own, especially as they were only boys, but there to watch nevertheless. There was an air of expectancy and the atmosphere was tense. The three boys felt stares upon them, but it was Will who received the most. Hatless now, his yellow hair blew in the cold wind and it was obvious he was no Spaniard. The crowd stood silently as the boys' crimes were read out. One man shouted that they were only doing their duty as enemies of the French, but he was quickly silenced by a French soldier, who felled him with a musket butt.

Will feigned indifference and looked around. Was Megan here? There were soldiers and … yes, there she was, sitting on a horse beside Major Deneuve and several other officers at the back of the crowd. She was looking straight at him and he could see the tears coursing down her face. He managed a small smile and mouthed the words, "I love you," but he thought she was probably too far away to see them. He wondered if Deneuve had spent the night with her and felt a surge of anger at the possibility, but there was nothing he could do about it now. It was all too late.

A man was prodding him, encouraging him to step down from the cart and he could see that the two boys already stood at the bottom of the gallows' steps. Awkwardly, he jumped from the cart and looked up. A man stood by one of the nooses, a big man, the hangman. He was not wearing French uniform, and Will wondered where Deneuve had found him.

Suddenly there was a commotion, and Antonio was barging through the crowd, his bound hands impeding his progress. Surprised, people moved out of his way, ignoring the shouts to stop him that came from the French officers. When he had a clear view of the cathedral ahead of him he started to run. He pelted for the great doors and possible sanctuary. People shouted, some, Will thought, shouting encouragement, but as Antonio ran up the steps there was a single shot and he fell forwards, then slid slowly down the steps to land in the dust of the plaza, blood trickling from a hole in his back. There was a shocked silence, then a moan, and Carmen was running towards him. She fell to her knees beside him, crying and moaning in Spanish. "What is she saying?" Will whispered to Juan who seemed stunned by the sudden turn of events and had stopped crying himself. "She say she sorry," Juan answered. "She say she had to do it." The puzzled boy looked into Will's eyes. "How could she do that? How could she betray her own brother?"

Will did not have an answer. Maybe when she had decided to tell Deneuve about Will, she had hoped to use her feminine whiles and get Deneuve to let Antonio go. Maybe she had not cared. Whatever the reason, her brother was dead and she was filled with regret now that it was too late. Will watched Carmen search the crowd to see who had fired the shot. Her eyes lit upon Major Deneuve astride his horse nearby. He was pocketing a pistol. She ran to him and pulled at his leg, screaming and shouting. "She say he promised to let Antonio go," said Juan quickly, translating her shouts. "She say she whored for him and he promised."

The crowd watched as Deneuve, angry and red-faced at her damning accusations, pushed her away with his foot and signalled for two of his men to take her away. Damn the girl! He would like to have shot her too, but there were already murmurings in the crowd, unhappy with the way Antonio had been dealt with, though Will thought that at least his death was quick. Carmen was dragged away, kicking and screaming.

"Get on with it, man!" said the French Colonel on the horse next to Deneuve. The French officer hurriedly signalled to the soldiers surrounding the boys. He could feel the tension of the crowd, like a tightly wound spring. Wanting to avoid trouble, he spoke quietly to a nearby lieutenant who then wheeled his horse around and rode to the cavalry detail that had brought the boys from their prison. Deneuve watched the troopers spread out around the crowd, effectively hemming them in on three sides, the cathedral making the fourth.

Will and Juan were prodded up the steps with a musket until they stood on the platform. Juan was shaking. "I'm sorry," said Will. It was his fault the youngster was about to lose his life. Juan looked at him, fear in his eyes, but said nothing. The hangman lifted the noose to put around his neck.

Suddenly there was a bang, and everyone's eyes turned to find the source of the noise, much closer than the guns firing from the city walls. As they did so, there was another. Two shots were fired. A woman screamed, and Will saw smoke from near the cathedral. A great surge of hope set the adrenaline coursing through his veins, and he head-butted the hangman in the stomach. Air escaped the man's mouth as he folded over, and Will kneed him in the face. "Run!" he shouted to Juan. There were other bangs, and French soldiers were responding to shouts from the mounted officers, running up the steps. Seeing their way barred, Will turned. "Jump!" he shouted to Juan and they both jumped from the back of the platform to land hard on the ground, people doing their best to get out of the way. Juan was already on his feet and running, pushing his way through the crowd before Will had found his feet. Deneuve was roaring at the crowd to catch them, but the people made a pathway and no one tried to stop them.

Then Will saw horses barring his way. The French cavalry. He stopped his headlong flight, looking left and right. Right. As he ploughed through more of the crowd a flaming bottle soared over his head and landed at a horse's feet, smashing and exploding with frightening force. Horse and rider screamed and people ran to get away. The plaza was in an uproar now. People milled about, shouting and screaming, horses and their riders tried to contain the crowd and reach Will and Juan at the same time. A blanket of gunpowder smoke hung over the square. Will could not see Juan, neither could he see Megan but he could see the entrance to one of the streets that led off the plaza, so he headed for it.

Suddenly a horse barred his way again. Major Deneuve sat astride it, his face a mask of anger and hatred. He had a sword in his hand. Roaring his anger, he slashed at Will but Will managed to step nimbly out of the way. The sword came down again and only just missed Will's head. He wondered for how long he could keep this up, dodging this way and that, trying to keep moving and out of the way of the deadly sword that kept slashing down. He knew that if he ran, Deneuve would follow and with his back to the man on the horse, he would have no chance of avoiding the sword.

Help came from an unexpected quarter. A black furry animal suddenly leapt in front of him and barked madly, snapping viciously at the horse's hooves. "Scrapper!" breathed Will, amazed. He had no time to wonder that the dog was alive, where he had come from, or where he had been all this time. Scrapper was forcing the horse backwards and though Deneuve was using his heels and crop, nothing would make the horse advance in the face of that snarling mouthful of bared teeth.

Will dodged to the left and saw Juan ahead of him, running down the street. He set off after him. There was chaos in the plaza. The cavalry horses were in the middle of the crowd who were deliberately impeding their progress. Scrapper ran with Will who heard a horse thundering down the narrow street, its hooves loud on the cobbles. Afraid that Deneuve had somehow managed to get out of the melee, Will ran faster but then a voice was calling his name and he stopped.

Megan brought the horse to a skidding halt and helped him up behind her. She cut the rope around his wrists with a knife. "Stolen," she explained briefly. Will grinned at her, then pointed to Juan, about to run round the corner in front of them. Megan urged the horse on, the sounds from the plaza fading away as they turned into the next street. There they caught up with Juan. Scrapper had already found him and he laughed when Will and Megan rode up. "See, he is alive!" he said, kneeling to embrace the dog.

Will laughed too, as pleased as Juan. "Come on up," he said and they pulled the boy onto the saddle between them and Will used the knife to cut his bonds.

"Where to?" asked Megan.

Where to indeed? Will knew they could not go back to the cellar now that Deneuve knew where it was. He could think of nowhere else unless ...

"We'll go back to your place," he said to Juan. "The room where they first caught us." And hope that no one else is living there, he thought as Juan guided them. He was almost certain that the French would have left it alone since their capture. It would seem that they had also left Scrapper who must have recovered after his knock on the head, and seemed none the worse for his experience. In fact he looked fatter and sleeker than when Will had last seen him and had obviously benefited from his time alone on the streets. He trotted along beside the horse with no limp at all, his wound completely healed.

They reached the dark alley and Will dismounted, leaving Megan and Juan on the horse. "If there's trouble, scarper," he said, then crept slowly to the door that was halfway along the wall. The door was half off its hinges and creaked when he pulled it aside. Inside, the room where the children had lived was deserted and filthy. The few belongings that they had left behind had been scattered and the mattresses torn. Will saw a rat scuttle across the floor. He went back outside.

"All clear," he said.

Megan and Juan dismounted and Will smacked the horse on the rump, sending it off up the street. He assumed a Frenchman would find it and it was too dangerous to keep. Meanwhile, Megan looked with distaste at the dirt and the lack of amenities. The state of the room made the cellar they had left seem positively palatial but she knew better than to complain. It was sanctuary for now – a place where they could rest and plan their next move.

Will scratched around on the shelves and in the corners but the food they had left behind had gone, or was spoilt by the rats and mice that had taken over. Hunger gnawed at his stomach and he tried to think when he had last eaten, but couldn't remember. He would have to hunt for food when it got dark, but at least they had a place to stay.

He found the butt of a candle lying on the floor but had no means of lighting it, so they sat in the dim room, uncertain what to do next.

"What made those bangs?" Megan asked, curled up with Will for warmth. Juan was searching the room for anything of value that they could use. It appeared that the children had one or two hiding places because he found a flint so they could light the candle. The room suddenly seemed less derelict in the small glow of the flame.

"I saw a bottle with a lighted wick," said Will in answer to Megan's question. "An' the first bangs were from near the cellar. I think it were Sarah an' the girls 'elpin' out."

"But what will happen to them? What if Deneuve realises it was them? He'll kill them!" said Megan, horrified to think what might happen to her friends.

It was something that had been worrying Will. He could only hope that they had not been seen starting the riot and that the chaos afterwards had kept them from being discovered. He wondered if he should go back to the plaza to see if they were all right. He suggested it to Megan and, unwillingly, she agreed. Part of her did not want to let Will out of her sight now that they were together again, but Sarah was her friend. Without her, she didn't know if she could have withstood all the trials of the war.

"What about my sisters?" said Juan, his small face stark with worry.

"If Sarah thought of the plan," Megan said, knowing that it must have been her, and not Amy who she doubted had the initiative to do so, "then she must have thought of a way to escape." She said this with more confidence than she felt, hoping it was true, then lapsed into an anxious silence.

"We 'ave ter get food," said Will eventually. Worrying about the girls was doing none of them any good. He stood up. "I'll go an' see what I can find and if I can, I'll go to the cellar."

Megan clung to him desperately. "Please be careful," she said. "I couldn't bear it if you were captured again."

"I promise."

Megan kissed him, then let him go. She knew that it would be useless asking to go with him. He would manage much better alone. "All right," she said, "but remember, if Deneuve sees you now, he'll kill you after all the trouble you've put him to, and he's probably told every soldier in Badajoz to be on the lookout for you. Take Scrapper. He won't want to be here without you anyway."

"I'm not likely to forget." Will kissed her gently again. "And I'll take Scrapper. He seems very capable of takin' care of 'imself. Aren't yer, boy?" He fondled the dog under the chin and Scrapper's tongue rasped against his hand. Will knew he was taking a risk by going out, but it was one he had to take. He hugged Megan close again. "Did Deneuve do anything to yer?" It was a question he had not wanted to ask, but he had to know the answer.

"No," she said, drawing back from him. She shuddered, remembering the touch of the Frenchman's fat fingers. "But I don't know for how long I could have held him off." She clung to him again.

"Thank God," said Will. "Now promise me you'll stay 'ere with Juan. I'll be back soon." She nodded. He kissed her hard on the mouth, then went to the door. "If yer 'ear anyone in the alley, snuff the candle," he said. By pushing hard he managed to get the door to close. He stared at it for a moment, then resolutely walked out of the alley with Scrapper at his heels.

Chapter 14

Out in the streets Will saw an uncommon amount of activity. Dusk was falling and French soldiers were everywhere, hurrying in the direction of the south walls. At first he thought they might be on the lookout for himself and his friends but then he realised that no one was taking any notice of civilians. He also realised something else. Preoccupied with his own problems, and so used to the ever-present sound of the artillery, he had not noticed the sudden upsurge in noise from the British guns and he wondered if they were close to making a breach. They had been pounding away at the south-eastern corner of the city walls for days now. Surely they must be on the verge of making an assault. The thought lifted his heart, for though he had had his misgivings when first setting eyes on the city, he had no doubt that Wellington and his engineers had thought things through and would manage to overcome the seemingly insurmountable difficulties.

As he hurried through the streets, he kept a watchful eye out for Major Deneuve. There was no doubt in his mind that the girls had been behind the diversion that had enabled himself and Juan to escape a hanging and he hoped that Deneuve had not seen where the first shots and bottles had come from. Would the girls still be in the cellar, or would they have gone somewhere else? He had to look, but first he wanted to see why the French were in such a dither.

By taking a roundabout route and following running Frenchmen, Will came to a place where the British artillery had smashed down a row of houses with a mis-placed cannon ball that had over-shot the wall. One house on the end still stood, leaning on the pile of rubble that had been its neighbours. Carefully, Will climbed onto the roof of the derelict house and, by lying flat, he was able to see what was going on.

What he saw plunged him to the depths of despair. The French, lit by oil lamps and flaming torches were busy bolstering the defences. Officers shouted commands to the hundreds of men who swarmed like ants over stone and soil, their voices raised in an effort to be heard above the pounding of the guns. He could see where the British had made three breaches but the French had dug trenches in the earth that protected the city wall, one above the other up the slope. If the British managed to get across them, there was an even tougher obstacle ahead. A huge ditch in front of the glacis had already been in front of the wall, but now it had been dug deeper and wider and it was filled with explosives, and wide planks of wood bristling with sword blades – *chevaux de frise*. The attackers would have to use ladders to cross the ditch, risk being blown up by the mines, and then have to try and force their way over sword blades and bits of iron, all the while with the French firing at them from above. It would be impossible. There was no way they could do it. Will stared at the breaches and wondered if Wellington knew what awaited his men. During the day, the guns still tore pieces of stone out of the wall, undoing the makeshift work that the French were doing at night to seal the gaps, and it was obvious that the General still saw this as his way into Badajoz, but it was equally obvious that there was no way he would get in without appalling loss of life. For a moment Will was glad that he was not going to be one of the soldiers taking part in the assault, but then he immediately chastised himself. He was part of the army and it was his job to join them, but there was no way he could. He thought of his friends; amiable Bob Tomkins and his girl-friend Molly, big Ron Parker, the ex-blacksmith, sharp-faced Nat Binns, a thief like himself, and his best pal, George Trim. Would he ever see them again? There was every chance that if they took part in the assault, they would be killed. Anger gripped him so hard that his knuckles whitened on the hands that held the edge of the roof. If that bastard Bordeaux had kept his thieving hands to himself, he would not have felt the need to go ahead of the army and he would not now be inside the city when he should be outside with his mates, taking the same risks they were. And he felt so impotent, knowing there was nothing he could do to prevent a terrible tragedy.

His mind was brought back to his own precarious situation by a growl from Scrapper. Will peered over the edge of the roof and saw yet more French soldiers approaching. Will ducked down, swearing under his breath, for leading them was Major Deneuve. Heart thumping he clung to the wood and straw that covered the part of the roof he lay on, and fervently hoped that Deneuve would not notice the dog. He heard the order to halt and Deneuve shouting out the soldiers' orders, then nothing. After a few minutes, Will risked a peep over the edge of the roof and saw Deneuve right below him deep in close conversation with another officer. Scrapper was hidden in shadows but Will could make out the hackles risen on his back. The dog knew that this man was the enemy. Slowly, Will slid on his stomach to a place where the roof had fallen in and let his legs drop through the hole.

There was quite a drop to the floor below but he held his breath and let go, landing in a heap, but without doing himself any damage. He found the doorway that was fortunately on the side away from Deneuve, and sidled round the wall until he was behind Scrapper. He touched the dog, who whirled round, startled, but when he saw it was Will, he wagged his tail and followed the beckoning finger round the back of the house and out of sight.

Will ran away from the scene of activity until he was sure Deneuve had seen nothing then walked breathlessly into the maze of streets that led to the cathedral plaza. He had taken much longer than anticipated already and Megan would be getting worried but he had to see if Maria, Sarah, and the others were all right. He came to the plaza where the cathedral brooded over the rain-washed cobbles. The gibbet was still there and Will shuddered to think how close he had come to hanging from it. Trying not to feel its brooding presence, he crept through the shadows to the cellar steps.

He entered the short tunnel that led to the cellar they had all lived in. It was quiet, and eerie. Heart in his mouth, afraid of what he might find, he stepped through the doorway into the room. It was dark. He could barely make out anything. "Sarah?" he called softly. "Are yer 'ere?" There was no reply. Silently he crossed the room and went into the next cellar, the one they had used to cook in. Here there was a faint light from the narrow opening at street level where a nearby torch flickered uncertainly, but he could smell that the fire had been lit recently.

"Sarah?" he called again. "Amy? Maria? It's me. Will."

He heard a shuffling sound from a hole in the wall that separated the cellar he was in from the next, and then a woman's shape stepped through into the dim light. "Will? Is that really you?" He recognised Sarah's voice, then he was embraced heartily. "Oh, Will! We didn't know if you'd managed to get away! Is Megan all right? And Juan? Oh, and you found Scrapper! How wonderful!" Sarah bent to stroke the dog, who wagged his tail in delight.

"'E found me," said Will. "And the others're fine. God, Sarah! I'm so glad the French didn't find yer! It were you as threw those bottles weren't it?"

"Yes," said Sarah. She had been joined now by Amy who was holding Rosa's hand, and Maria with the baby. They were all smiling. "We had to do something to help you, Will," Sarah continued. "We were just lucky we had suitable materials to hand. Maria and I threw the bottles while Amy fired the muskets."

"Well, thanks. All of yer. Didn't fancy 'avin' me neck stretched. Neither did Juan." He embraced them one by one.

"Pity about Antonio," he said soberly. "'E were a good lad. Can't understand 'ow Carmen could throw 'im ter the wolves like that. Though I know why she betrayed me." He felt a blush reddening his face as he glanced at Maria. Sarah and Amy looked puzzled and it was obvious Maria had said nothing to them about Carmen's reasons.

"Why did ... ?" Sarah started to ask but Will was unwilling to go into things now and headed her off.

"And afterwards?" he said quickly. "Ow did yer manage ter get away without 'em seein' yer?"

"Once the French panicked, the crowd helped by getting into the way of the soldiers and horses and we slipped back here," said Sarah. "We've been hiding in the next cellar most of the time, but no one's been near."

"Maybe they won't bother tryin' ter find yer," said Will and he told them of all the activity he had seen by the breaches. "I think they've got a lot on their minds right now and maybe our men'll be attackin' soon. Megan and Juan are back at yer old 'ouse, Maria. The French've bin there and taken what they wanted, but it's not so bad. I'm supposed ter be out lookin' for food but I 'ad ter come and see if yer were all right."

"We 'ave food," said Maria. "There eez still some left." She gave the baby to Sarah and immediately started to gather up what they had.

"You'd best all come wi' me," said Will. "Yer'll be safer out of 'ere." He helped Maria bundle everything they could possibly use into the rags of clothing that littered the cellar and then led them to the cellar steps. He peered out into the plaza, but everything was still quiet. "Come on!" he whispered, and they stepped out into the shadows.

They reached the small house without difficulty but as soon as Will entered he was buffeted by Megan's fists. He caught and held them, and dragged her into a dark corner while Maria hugged Juan fiercely, speaking to him in rapid Spanish, and the two older girls stashed away the things they had brought from the cellar. "What's the matter?" he said, quietly, amazed at the reception she had given him.

"You were gone so long I thought something had happened to you," she said. She looked up at him and tears pricked her lashes. She flung his hands away and furiously wiped her eyes with her sleeve. She knew the strain was getting to her, and the thought that Will might have been captured again had tied her stomach into knots of worry.

"I'm sorry," said Will and pulled her rigid body close to him. He pushed strands of damp hair from her eyes and kissed her softly on the forehead.

Megan buried her head in his shoulder. She had been aching with anxiety and knew he was right to have gone back to the cellar, but oh, how she wished they were away from all this, back in the camp with their friends and her uncle. She gave a big sigh, glad to feel his strength and protection once again.

"I'm 'ungry," said Will, hoping to deflect her mournful mood into something more practical. "Let's see what food we 'ave."

They made a meal of wizened apples, hard cheese and crusts of bread, not much but enough to still the hunger pangs. After that they lay squashed together on the two torn mattresses. Megan lay as close as she could to Will, listening to the rats and mice scrabbling in the corners, hoping that they would not crawl on her in the night, and already itching from the fleas and bed-bugs in the mattress. Despite the excitement of the day and the worry of the previous night, sleep did not come easily. Her mind went back again to her life at Camberwell Hall. Though it had only been seven months, it seemed a lifetime ago. It felt as though she had been living like a pauper for ever. She tried to think of her wardrobe of silk and satin dresses, baths of hot water and scented soap, a soft mattress and cool sheets, and what it was like to have a full stomach, but found she had quite forgotten how any of those things felt. Tears pricked her eyelids once more and she wondered if she would ever go back to that lifestyle again.

It was just too disturbing to think about the past, so she thought instead of the present, and wondered, as she had many times since it happened, why Carmen had betrayed them to the French. Was it because they were English? She knew Carmen disliked her, but it had seemed an unreasonable dislike, for it had not extended to Sarah or Amy. She had also noticed her staring at Will when she thought no one was looking. A sudden idea came to her, and she wondered why she had not thought of it before. Could it be that jealousy was the reason she had informed on them? Maybe Carmen had fancied Will and did not like her because she was Will's girl. Her arm stretched out over Will's hard stomach. He lay on his back, already asleep, exhausted. It struck her that this was the first time they had lain together since they had declared their love, but though she lay beside him, Will had not tried anything untoward. It would have been difficult to do so anyway with Sarah and Amy squashed next to her. The thought made her giggle and she stifled her mouth in Will's shirt. What would she do if he did try to make love to her? Sometimes she ached with longing for his touch, and the feelings he engendered in her made her rather guilty and embarrassed. Was it normal to feel like that about a man? She was so inexperienced in the ways of love, yet she had seen the looks Will received from other women and thought that maybe they experienced the same feelings she did.

Could it be that Carmen was in love with Will too? They had spent a day or two in each others' company before she, Sarah, and Amy had been rescued. Could they have formed a relationship in that time? Surely not. But then Carmen was pretty, and there had been that whore in the mountain village. Juanita. Will had bedded her, and Megan had well learned that soldiers had needs. Was it possible?

Now that the thought had entered her head, Megan could not get rid of it. She would have to find out, but how? Could Will be trusted to tell the truth, if there was any to tell? Who else would know?

Her thoughts were interrupted by a small cry from Carlotta, and Maria hushing her. She heard the girl get off the other mattress and pour a little water onto a rag that she twisted into a knot for the child to suck. Carefully, Megan managed to get off the mattress without waking Will, and she tip-toed to Maria who was rocking the baby back to sleep.

Maria smiled at her in the dim light from the candle. "She gets the teeth," she murmured quietly. "The pain it wakes her."

Megan nodded. The floor was cold on her bare feet and she shivered. She could hear distant shouting, but the only sound in the room was the even breathing of the sleepers. "Maria, I have to ask you something," she whispered. "Does Carmen like Will?"

Surprised by the question and uncertain how to answer, Maria rocked the baby to give herself time to think. She liked this brave girl, but she did not want to make trouble for Will whom she liked even more.

"It is possible," she said evasively. "'Oo would not?"

"I mean, does she like him like I do?" Megan tried again. "When Sarah, Amy and I were imprisoned, did she try anything with him?" She paused, then said, "Did you see him kiss her?"

"No," said Maria truthfully. "I did not see that." She turned her head away, afraid that if Megan asked more pointed questions, she would have to tell the truth about what she had heard and seen that night in the room at Deneuve's headquarters. She felt Megan's eyes on her. "I did not see 'im kiss 'er," she repeated. "Now Carlotta must go to bed." She turned towards the mattress where her brother and sister lay sound asleep.

Megan studied her back for a moment more and then nodded. She had the distinct feeling that Maria was hiding something. She was just walking back to her own bed when the broken door was flung open. Megan screamed, starting the baby wailing, and Scrapper barking. Everyone woke up, startled by the sudden noise.

"Will! You are 'ere! You must 'ide me!"

Will was already on his feet, the musket in his hands. "Carmen?" Surely it was her shouting. The baby yelled louder. Will squinted in the poor light. Carmen was standing in the doorway.

"Carmen? What the 'ell do yer want? 'Ave yer brought soldiers?" he asked angrily.

Carmen shook her head. "No. I run away from the French Major," said Carmen. "'E is disgusting. But 'e look for me. I come 'ere to 'ide. I know this place where Maria and Juan live. I not know you are 'ere. But you are." She smiled. "Will! Remember our night together. You must 'ide me."

Megan's stomach churned and she felt sick. So she had been right. Anger welled up inside her but she was so choked up she could not speak. She looked at Will who was staring at Carmen as though she was from another planet.

"Yer out of yer mind!" he said savagely, so annoyed that Carmen had the gall to ask for help that he did not realise Megan must have heard the incriminating words. "Yer the one 'oo showed Deneuve the cellar! Yer betrayed Juan and me! And got yer brother killed too! Yer must be mad if yer think I'll do anythin' ter 'elp yer! Now get out! An' if yer lead Deneuve 'ere, so 'elp me, I'll kill yer!"

He pointed the musket menacingly towards her. Carmen tried a wheedling, pleading look but the musket was held in steady hands and aimed at her heart and she knew he meant what he said. She cast a look at Megan and her eyes narrowed. She knew how to get her own back. If this girl and Will had not got back together, things might have worked out differently. Now it was too late. She had got her brother killed, was alone in the world. She was a soldier's whore, and probably always would be.

"'E is not the man you think 'e is, *senorita*," she said viciously to Megan. "I sleep with him. I ..." But she got no further for Megan suddenly found her voice and her wits. She snatched up the other musket and aimed it at the girl. "Get out!" she shrieked. "Get out!" Carmen stared at her in alarm, saw her finger tighten on the trigger, and turned quickly. The musket fired and the sound was deafening. The girls screamed and coughed as smoke filled the room, the baby wailed and Will grabbed hold of Megan's arm though the musket was now empty. All stared at the doorway, expecting to see Carmen's body on the floor but when the smoke drifted away there was nothing but a splintered door jamb and Carmen was gone.

Megan stared at Will, her eyes filled with anger and tears. "You bastard!" she said. "You slept with her! I can't believe you'd do that to me! I thought you loved me!"

"I do!" Will held out his arms in supplication, but she backed away.

"Don't touch me!" she shouted angrily. "Get out! I never want to see you again!" Her eyes blazed at him and he stared at her, dumbfounded, not knowing what to say because it was true. He had betrayed her trust for a moment's pleasure and it had come back to haunt him. With the musket still in his hand, he turned around quietly, and left the room.

Megan watched him go, then sank down onto the mattress, put her head in her hands, and sobbed as though she would never stop.

Chapter 15

Evening – 6th April 1812

Private George Trim crouched in the mud and waited for the order to attack. All around him were the small sounds of men shifting from one uncomfortable position to another, whispered words of advice, and even some quiet jocularity, but there was something very strange about the night. It was too quiet. For days there had been the sound of the big guns pounding the walls of Badajoz and its forts. Now they were silent. George's bowels were empty and he hadn't eaten since noon, but the poor food had not gone down well and his insides churned. Having gone through this once before at Ciudad Rodrigo he had thought that maybe this time would not be so bad, but now he knew what to expect it was worse. Much worse. And waiting for something to happen was the worst part of all. He glanced to his left where Bob Tomkins crouched next to Ron Parker and Nat Binns. All looked stoney-faced, emotionless, their eyes on the city they had come to besiege, but George knew that they were as frightened as he was. He too turned his gaze towards the towering walls of Badajoz, lit only by braziers in the gun emplacements, and at the dark, ragged holes in that wall, holes made by the British guns. A scree of broken stone was piled on the sloping glacis that led to the breaches, stone that had been knocked out of the wall by the artillery. Stone that was supposed to help them climb up that slope. But before the slope of rubble was a very deep, watery ditch. A ditch with no bridge. Some of the soldiers to his right carried ladders. They seemed very flimsy and he wondered whether they would break under the weight of the hundreds of soldiers who would have to use them. It was very dark, and they had been here for over two hours already, waiting. The attack was supposed to have started at seven-thirty but there had been delays. Now, he thought, it must be getting on for ten. Soldiers shifted their weight, cramping in the cold. George imagined the French soldiers on top of the wall and in the gun emplacements. Could they see the mass of British soldiers waiting? He and his colleagues had crossed the Rivillas stream that ran between the trenches they had dug and the city itself, leaving behind the flooded part of the stream that spread to the east. Now they were in front of the breaches and soon they would have to make an assault. He wished

Wellington would give the order to attack. This waiting was awful and he tried not to think that these moments might be his last.

Seven thousand five hundred men waited around him. Another four thousand men of the 3rd Division under General Picton had been sent to storm the castle, and General Leith's 5th Division was close by the River Guadiana on the western side of the city, ready to attack the San Vincente bastion. Rumour had it that Wellington was hoping that by attacking in three places at once, it would divert some of the French from the breaches. George wondered if another rumour he had heard was true – that half the French garrison was waiting at the breaches for the assault. The British were said to have many more men, but all knew that the defenders had the advantage.

"Wish they'd bloody well get on with it," muttered Nat Binns, voicing all their thoughts. Anything was better than waiting with your stomach heaving, thinking about what was about to happen.

As if in answer to Nat's wish, the sky was suddenly lit up to the north by a burning straw bale that had been thrown down on the castle side. Judging by the shouts and rattle of musket fire, followed closely by the thunder of artillery, the attackers there had been discovered. Close by, George heard the shouted order to attack given by several officers at once and he moved forward in the darkness with the others towards the ditch, his legs stiff, and with hands clutching his bayoneted musket so tightly he thought the sweat would stick them to it. There was another flurry of gunfire from the castle, and then the awful sound of explosions as the British set off concealed mines.

The French were not stupid. Expecting an attack from the castle side, and knowing there would be one at the breaches, they lit up the night with flaming straw and suddenly it was as light as day, the sudden brightness dazzling. George was jostled by men eager to get to the fight and he was almost pushed from a ladder into the ditch. He tried to steady himself but was then hurled backwards as the first men down set off the mines. Splattered with bits of flesh and dirt, he gagged. A man landed on top of him, his arm ripped off and one side of his face blown away. There were more explosions, and screams, then he was pulled to his feet and pushed onwards, across the ditch. Water and mud caught hold of him so that he struggled towards the other side. Wounded men drowned as they were pushed down by others. Only one ladder remained intact, bending beneath the weight of men. He trod on a body. The dead and wounded in the ditch made a bridge and George tried not to think about who he might be stumbling on. Already he had lost sight of Nat, Bob and Ron but the men beside him went grimly forward.

He managed to get to the other side of the ditch but then found his way blocked by iron spikes, a wall of stones, and, further up the glacis, the *chevaux de frise*. Musket fire came constantly from the ramparts above. Shells exploded and canister from hidden gun emplacements enfiladed the breaches. The noise was terrible. Fires had started all along the dryer parts of the ditch, crackling amongst wood thrown there for the purpose, and fanned by the small wind. The wounded, unable to move and desperate to escape the flames, cried out in anguish as clothes and flesh caught fire, but men were forced onwards and no one helped. A man further along screamed briefly as canister set off a barrel of gunpowder hidden in the mud. The scream was abruptly cut off as his body parts shot up in the air, while men close by died or lost limbs. Stunned, George found himself falling down into the ditch again, covered in blood.

For a moment he could do nothing, deafened by the noise and unsure where he was, then, gradually, he became aware that his right arm hurt. Lying on top of a dead man, he stared uncomprehendingly at his sleeve. It was darker than the rest of his jacket. He had lost his musket and couldn't move. His legs seemed to be under something heavy. Looking down at them he saw they were covered by two more bodies. While carnage raged around him, he slowly pushed at the bodies and managed to shove them off his legs, then got onto his knees. Ahead, more men were clambering across the bridge of bodies and were trying with their bare hands to remove the sword blades projecting from the thick wooden planks but no one as yet had reached the breaches. Men were falling back all the time, hit by canister and muskets fired at short range, impaled by the sword blades as they were pushed from behind. Sergeants and officers shouted, urging men on, and despite the appalling casualties, groups of men were obeying them, though they could hardly be heard in the tumult. The men grunted, prayed, shouted, yelled, cheered, screamed – anything to give themselves courage. In an effort to reach the breaches, and with men pushing from behind, those falling onto the sword blades provided another bridge for those coming after. The screams were terrible to hear and George, still trying to gather his scattered wits, wondered if there would be any British soldiers left if this carried on. He was knocked flat again by a man trampling across the bodies and he fell forward into some unmentionable muck. Lifting his head he spat and then retched, vomit spewing out of his mouth onto a dead man with both his legs missing. Wiping his mouth on the back of his hand, his other arm hanging useless by his side, he staggered to his feet, slipped on his own vomit and ploughed forward only to fall again when the man ahead of him keeled over backwards, felled by a musket ball. He was deafened once more by another explosion and wondered if he couldn't just stay where he was. His arm hurt and he was beginning to feel light-headed, but then Angus McKay, a sergeant and veteran of many battles, suddenly appeared by his side.

"Get up, yon sassenach bastard," sneered the Scotsman. "Hidin' away are yer?" He pushed George to his unsteady feet and prepared to go on, then lost his footing and fell onto one of the iron spikes that projected from the edge of the ditch. He screamed and George stared at the bloody point sticking from McKay's back without really realising what had happened. Everything was becoming blurry and the terrible noise seemed to be fading away. He toppled backwards onto a cushion of bodies and sank into oblivion.

*

Will was back in the plaza when he suddenly saw the light in the sky by the castle and heard the cheers and shouts of thousands of men, seemingly from all sides of the city. The assault had begun! Explosions and gunfire came from north and south. Angry and upset after his argument with Megan, he had planned to go back to the cellar, if only to give himself time to think what to do next. Now he had other things to think about and he knew what he must do. Somehow he had to help the British get into Badajoz. But what could he do, alone, and with only a musket? He fished in his pocket and brought out three cartridges and a small amount of powder. Four bullets, counting one already in the gun he had reloaded. The plaza was deserted but by listening carefully he could make out that the attack was on three fronts. The breaches he could do nothing about and he trembled to think of the carnage that the French must be wreaking on the British at that point. The attackers were also at the castle, presumably with ladders. The main French arsenal was there. Perhaps that was his best bet.

With Scrapper at his heels, he hurried through the streets until he came within sight of the castle. He scrambled up the hillside, listening to the shouts, screams, and explosions that came from the other side of the walls. He well knew that the French had barricaded the main gates into the castle but he remembered the small portal through which he had entered himself when looking for food. In the darkness that covered the city side of the castle, he crept round to the door and found it guarded by two soldiers. They looked pretty relaxed, probably because they assumed that the castle was well defended and did not anticipate taking any physical part in the battle. Both men carried muskets. Will suddenly heard the sound of marching feet. Pushing Scrapper, he and the dog stepped back into the shadows of the bushes and watched a detachment of French soldiers demand entrance to the castle. The sight of the reinforcements gave Will hope that maybe the British were having some success with the assault, but he could not hear any cheers now, only screams and bangs.

When the French soldiers had gone inside, Will waited until the two guards, brought to attention briefly by the French commander, settled down again, and then took careful aim. The musket banged, smoke wreathed his face and before it had even cleared he had reloaded. He fired again, and when he looked, both soldiers were down. One stirred feebly for a moment but then he was still.

Two bullets gone. Two left. Will reloaded the musket, and frisked the dead guards for more cartridges. He found some and stuffed them in his pocket together with a horn of powder, then he opened the door and entered the castle. Seeing nobody, but hearing plenty of noise from both inside and out, he found the room that held the small arms. When he had last seen it, the room had contained several thousand muskets, barrels of powder, and box after box of cartridges. Now it was nearly empty. He was not to know that each man on the ramparts above the breaches had been given eight loaded muskets, and that exploding powder barrels were contributing to the carnage there.

While Scrapper sniffed around, Will rummaged amongst the scattered boxes and found a few more cartridges and a little spilt powder that he scooped up and added to his collection. Feeling more confident, he made his way stealthily to the central courtyard of the castle and peered round a wall. There he found a hive of noisy activity. French soldiers were running up the stone staircases onto the battlements with ammunition, water, straw bales, and lighted torches. Barrels of gunpowder, cannon shot and canister were stacked ready for use. A quick look told Will that there were few casualties, a fact that boded ill for the British attackers whom he assumed were trying to scale the cliff and castle wall. Judging by the amount of gunfire from the battlements, they were having a hard time of it.

He wondered what to do. He must provide a diversion, something to take some of the attention away from the British. He went back through a doorless opening and went from room to room, looking for something, anything, he could use.

In one of the rooms was a cannon. It had seemingly been facing a hole in the castle wall that looked out over the Rivillas stream, but now it was turned around so that it faced an inside wall. There it stood, complete with limber, cannon shot, fuses, linstock, rammer, even a water bucket. It was a small gun, only a four pounder, and he thought that was maybe why it was not being used on the walls. An idea came to him. Powder, he needed powder. He looked in the box that held the cannon balls and shot. There was one bag of powder. He grinned.

Taking the bag and a ball, he carefully loaded the gun. Now he needed a flame. Taking up the linstock he crept through the rooms, back to the central courtyard. There small fires burned. The French had used them to light the first straw bales and torches so they could see what they were doing. Everybody was far too busy to notice him. He poked the long stick into the flames, and ran back with it to the gun.

Quickly he pricked the powder bag, stuffed in a long fuse, and lit it. Then he dropped the linstock and ran.

He was outside the castle and running down the hillside with a joyful Scrapper, who thought it was all a game, by the time the fuse burned down to the powder but the resulting explosion still knocked him off his feet and set the dog barking madly. Breathless, he heard the first screams. The cannon ball had shot through the intervening walls and across the castle courtyard, ripping through barrels of gunpowder on its way. The barrels shattered, spraying great gouts of powder onto the fires. The explosions rocked the castle as the ball carried on through the outer wall on Will's left, to bounce harmlessly down the hillside towards the River Guadiana. But the job had been done. The castle walls, though reinforced by the French in places, were old and weathered. Now the ones the cannon ball passed through, helped by the explosions of gunpowder, fell and buried French soldiers, raising an enormous cloud of dust. Watching, Will laughed out loud. It had turned out even better than he had hoped. Now the French had other things on their minds than the assault on the castle walls.

*

General Picton and the 3rd Division who had been ordered to take the castle, had indeed been having a hard time. Every time they had erected ladders and men had climbed up, they had been forced back and were now blood-slicked and weary. Piles of bodies clustered at the bottom of the cliff and Picton wondered if he would ever manage to breast the walls. Wounded himself, he gathered his remaining men for one last effort, and then the explosions began. Realising they were coming from inside the castle and were not aimed at his forces, he gave a joyful shout and urged his men on. The rickety ladders went up one more time and although some of the French soldiers still remained on the battlements, the British were now able to reach the top and to gain access to the castle.

A great cheer rang out as the first men went over the top. More men eagerly followed, easily clearing the battlements of the few French soldiers who remained there, and the castle was soon taken. Men scurried down the stone steps into the cloud of dust in the courtyard that was being blown away in skeins by the wind and where Frenchmen staggered in numb disbelief, or lay moaning in their own blood.

Will ran back through the small doorway and met a Colonel coughing in the smoke and dust. The Colonel had men behind him and barely took any notice of Will, thinking him to be a Spanish street urchin, until the boy took his arm and said, "This way, sir." The English voice startled the Colonel but he followed Will out through the door, onto the hillside and into fresh air.

"Sergeant! Form the men up!" he bellowed to an NCO following close behind. The Colonel knew that if he did not hold the men in close discipline from the first, they would run riot through the city and there were still things to be done. Judging by the awful noise coming from the breaches, the attack there had failed, but cheering coming from the direction of the San Vincente bastion suggested that Leith's 5th Division was having some success.

Colonel Foot took a closer look at his guide and the dog beside him. Now that he could see him better in the light of the castle flames, it was clear that this boy was not Spanish. For a start the hair that stuck out from under the grubby hat was the colour of dirty corn, and his eyes were blue. "You're English!" he said, surprised. "Who are you?"

"Private Will Tucker, sir," said Will, standing up straighter and saluting. "Fourth Kent Light Infantry. Captain Camberwell's Company, sir."

"Good Lord! What on earth are you doing here, lad? How did you get in?"

"Long story, sir. Here ter rescue my girl. Captain Camberwell's niece, sir," answered Will.

Colonel Foot suddenly remembered a tale that had run through the

English camp of a servant who had gone on ahead of the army in order to rescue a lady. "You are Camberwell's servant?" he enquired.

"Yes, sir."

Foot looked back at the castle. Screams and shouts pierced the dust clouds as the British finished off the French survivors. "Did you have something to do with that explosion?" he said.

"Sort of, sir. Fired a cannon, but it must've caught some powder on the way. Did the trick though, sir. Yer got in."

The Colonel smiled and put a hand on Will's shoulder. "We certainly did. And now we have to go help those poor bastards at the breaches. Show us the way, lad."

*

Wellington had heard the massive explosion at the castle and seen the huge dust cloud and flames that followed it. He prayed silently for his men, assuming that the French had set off a series of mines, but now his attention was taken by the fight at the breaches. The battle there was the worst he and his generals had ever seen. The slaughter was horrific. There were piles of bodies in the ditch, on the slope of stones, impaled on the *chevaux de frise* and at the breaches themselves, yet still small groups rallied to heroic commanders and ploughed on. It was however, a lost cause. The walls remained defended. Reluctantly he gave the order for retreat, knowing he had lost. Bugles sounded, and those who could staggered back across the mountains of bodies, exhausted, numb and just glad to be alive. Seeing the British retreating, Badajoz's guns stopped firing.

Sadly watching his soldiers stumbling away from the city walls, Wellington knew now that their only chance lay in capturing the castle, but while his thoughts were willing General Picton to perform this unlikely miracle he heard the faint sound of joyous bugles and cheers from the far side of the city. His heart leapt with sudden hope. Had General Leith been successful in capturing the San Vincente bastion?

"Sir! Sir!"

Wellington turned to see a horse galloping towards him, its hooves spewing mud in all directions. The rider was gesticulating wildly with one hand while trying to control the horse with the other.

"Sir! The castle! It's been taken!" The soldier was grinning from ear to ear as the horse slewed to a stop beside the General. Quick words followed, and Wellington felt a great surge of renewed hope.

At that moment cheers, shots, and screams came from much closer at hand. Quickly putting his telescope to his eye, he studied the French soldiers on the ramparts who, just a few minutes before, were scathingly jeering the British retreat. Now they were turned away from him, and yes, some were engaged in hand to hand fighting. It could only mean one thing. The assaults on the castle and the San Vincente had been successful and the British were inside the city!

He roared out the order to attack the breaches again. The surprised remnants of the 4th and Light Companies were commanded to turn around and go back towards the hell they were gladly moving away from, only to find that this time the ramparts above the breaches were empty and silent. The realisation that they were getting help from the inside gave the tired men renewed strength and vigour. Cheering wildly, they scrambled up the stone scree and swarmed over the walls.

Chapter 16

The British soldiers rushed through the breaches and over the ramparts, hampered by the piles of dead and wounded, but eager to get at the French who had caused them such misery and fear. The fight on the city side of the walls was short and brutal, the British maddened with rage. Although many of the French surrendered, they were shown no mercy. Officers tried to hold the soldiers in some sort of discipline but it was hopeless. Once the men were past the defenders, all hell broke loose.

There followed an orgy of drunkenness, whoring, and killing that made the aftermath of Ciudad Rodrigo seem like a picnic. Let loose in the city, angry that the battle to get there had been so terrible, the British soldiers took their revenge on the populace who had harboured the enemy. Wine shops and taverns were the first places to suffer and it was not long before nearly every soldier was drunk and on the rampage for women and loot. The screams of the French soldiers were soon added to as girls, and even old women, were raped by the British who took what they wanted. The officers could do nothing against this unstoppable force and some even sympathised. Drink, women, and plunder were the soldiers' reward.

Will fought the French alongside Colonel Foot, using his musket as a club, knocking down Frenchmen with abandon, glad to be doing something positive for his own side. As more men poured through the breaches and the French began to surrender, he stood and caught his breath, the now broken musket dangling from one tired hand. He wondered where Scrapper had got to. The dog had been barking and trying to bite the ankles of anyone he could reach, both French and British alike, and Will hoped that he had not annoyed someone to the point of murder.

"Will!" The voice that shouted his name came from a few yards away. Will looked for the owner and his face broke into a huge grin. A very sweaty and dirty-faced Nat Binns stood over a dead Frenchman, waving his musket, the smile on his face matching that of his friend. Nat scrambled over the body and strode towards him on his bandy legs before enveloping Will in a hug that nearly squeezed the breath out of him.

"Shit a brick, lad, but it's good ter see yer!" said Nat. "I knew the Frenchies wouldn't 've got yer!" Nat stood back and grinned at him, then was almost bowled over by Scrapper, who mistakenly took Nat for one of the enemy. "Jesus! Don't tell me this is that blasted mongrel yer found? Geroff me, yer daft bugger!" Nat wrestled in a friendly way with the dog until Will gave a word of command and Scrapper stopped trying to drag Nat to the ground by the tattered sleeve of his dirty red jacket.

"Where are the others? George? Bob? Ron?" After the pleasure of seeing his old friend, Will realised that that Nat was alone and he was worried.

The smile left Nat's face. "Dunno, lad. We got separated in the breaches. It was a God-awful fight. Bodies everywhere." For a moment both were silent. There was a very real possibility that their friends were dead. Will stared around him, at the French bodies and the grim British who were looting the dead and, in some cases, bayoneting the wounded. Flame light flickered on their faces, giving them a hellish red glow and he knew he could not stand and watch.

"Let's go find 'em," he said grimly. Nat, seeing squads of cheering soldiers making their way into the dark streets, was tempted by the thought of the liquor and female companionship awaiting him there, but knew he also would not rest until his friends were accounted for. He nodded and followed Will through the nearest smoking hole in the wall.

Both stopped and stared in horror at the devastation of the breaches. Everywhere they looked were piles of bloody and charred bodies and limbs. Fire flickered in the ditch where screams told of wounded men being burned alive, though now officers had men forming bucket chains from the stream and were attempting to put the fires out. Feeble moans came from nearby as some of the wounded moved and called for help. Blood was everywhere, shining darkly crimson in the fire-light. Will had seen the carnage of war before at Ciudad Rodrigo but the awful sight made him sick to his stomach, and he wondered how on earth they would find anyone in these inhuman piles. Yet search they must. He took a deep breath to steady his nerves, then scrambled back up to the ramparts and took a torch from its niche before climbing down to Nat who still stood as though he had taken root.

"Come on," he said bleakly. Holding the torch high in front of him, he started to make his way over the heaps. Nat slowly followed.

They found Bob Tomkins first. The boy lay half in and half out of the ditch, his head and shoulders on the rim, his legs caught by the twisted remnants of one of the ladders. Eyes closed, he had a neat bullet hole in his neck and a shattered arm. Tears ran slowly down Will's cheeks as he removed Bob from the ladder as gently as he could. This poor, bloody wreck was far removed from the laughing youth who poked his nose into everyone else's business, yet was a cheerful and amusing companion. Will wondered how he would be able to tell Molly, Bob's girl, that her beau was dead. Silently, he and Nat laid the youth on the edge of the ditch atop another corpse and continued to look for Ron and George. Will was very afraid of what they might find.

Half an hour later they were thankfully joined by big Ron Parker who, like Nat, had been fighting inside the city but had had the same idea, to look for his friends. He had sustained a slight bullet wound in the thigh that was making him limp, but it was only a scratch and had stopped bleeding so he was ignoring it. After the first glad greetings, the three continued the search. They had been pulling dead and wounded men aside for more than an hour before they found George Trim. At first Will thought his friend was dead. The boy was still and his face was white but when he dragged a body from George's legs, there came a faint groan. "Faster!" said Will, the adrenaline pumping now that he realised George was alive. Nat held the torch while he and Ron pushed and pulled at bodies and stones until they could free George and carry him away from the carnage.

They laid him down on a bare piece of ground near the stream and saw his bloody arm. It seemed to be the only wound but George had obviously lost a lot of blood. He would have died if the dead man next to him had not been wedged so tightly that his body had pressed hard on the wound and stopped the bleeding. Will shouted to two passing bandsmen whose job it was to take the wounded back to the surgeons, but they waved him away. They were already trying to man-handle a make-shift stretcher and could not help.

"The bastards'll be sacking the town," muttered Ron as he heaved the unconscious George onto his wide shoulder.

Megan! All of a sudden Will's thoughts flew to her and the others in Maria's small house. What would happen to them when the British soldiers reached that part of town? He knew full well. He grabbed hold of Nat's arm. "Where's the Captain?" he demanded. "Where's Camberwell?"

"'E's with Wellington," answered Nat. surprised at Will's sudden vehemence. "'E couldn't fight 'cos of 'is ankle."

So much had happened since he had left the British camp, Will had forgotten all about Richard Camberwell's broken ankle. Quickly he told the others that Megan, Sarah, and Amy had been found and where they were, naming the street and describing the alley. "If they're not there, they might've gone back to the cellar. It's under the building with the broken green door, to the right of the cathedral in the plaza. Tell the Captain. I'm going back to get 'em," he said. "You take George to the doc. I'll see yer later."

"Take care, Will," warned Ron. "It's going to be bad in there and our lads are as likely to kill you as the French, especially 'cos you have no uniform. They'll shoot first and ask questions later, like as not." Will knew that Ron was right. He remembered Ciudad Rodrigo and suspected that this night and the following days would be worse.

"I 'ave ter go," he said simply. "The girls'll stand no chance if the bastards get to 'em before I do."

"We'll see George right and round up some of the men ter come an' 'elp yer," said Nat, though even as he said it, he wondered how they were to find men from their Company in the hell that was Badajoz that night. Will nodded and shook them both by the hand. Scrapper barked his own farewell and both boy and dog turned back to the city.

Ron was right. It was bad. The scene inside the city was as chaotic and bloody as outside. Will and Scrapper scrambled over stones and bodies. Houses had been demolished by British artillery. Spanish citizens who had mistakenly thought they could protect their properties and their women folk lay dead, and French soldiers had been bayoneted for the few trifles they hid in the seams of their jackets. Will could hear the screams and shouts, see the flames leaping up from buildings torched by the invading army, smell the blood and roasting flesh, the dung, the woodsmoke. The streets teemed with rats, disturbed from their hiding places by the noise and activity. Horses galloped aimlessly, frightened and riderless. Will saw an officer trying to organise a group of men into some sort of order, then watched as one of the soldiers felled the officer with the butt of his rifle before leading the cheering men down the street at a run. Will recognised the officer. It was Colonel Foot.

"Colonel!" he said, helping the officer to his feet, "Are yer all right, sir?"

Foot looked bewildered for a moment, rubbing his bleeding cheek, then recovered some of his wits. "Er, yes. I think so." He frowned at Will, and winced. "I'll have Baker on a charge for that if he survives the night!" He looked puzzled for a moment, then his face cleared. "Ah, yes. Tucker. You're the one who helped us in. Right?"

"Yes, sir." Will started to turn away, his thoughts with Megan, but the officer stopped him with a hand on his arm. "Where are you going?"

"There are people I 'ave ter get to," said Will. He whistled for Scrapper who was sniffing at a very interesting pile of unmentionable filth. The dog trotted towards him somewhat reluctantly.

"Can I help?" The Colonel knew that trying to stop the army from its depredations was useless, but he wanted to be doing something. Will paused for thought. Maybe having an officer with him might help if he encountered any opposition. At least the man had a sword. Quickly he explained about the girls and children holed up in Maria's derelict house. "Best get to 'em, then, lad," said the Colonel, his face set in hard lines. "If this rabble gets there first, there's no knowing what might happen."

As they hurried through the streets, the Colonel with his sword drawn, and Will picking up a loaded musket from a fallen soldier on the way, Will felt the worry gnaw at his insides. What if he was too late?

Their way was blocked several times and they had to take many detours. Bands of marauding soldiers, some wearing stolen civilian clothes and most carrying skins of wine or bottles of brandy, filled the alleys and streets. Screams came from houses as they battered down doors to find the women. Colonel Foot was often tempted to try and prevent the looting and raping but Will knew that the man would be injured or worse if he stopped to help the occupants or discipline the soldiers. The only man who could contain them was Wellington himself, and it would surely take him a long time to restore order. Colonel Foot was of more help to Will at the moment and he determined that the officer should stay close. It seemed to be a good idea as no one bothered them though they passed many drunken and whoring men.

They managed to avoid trouble and finally reached the alleyway that contained Maria's hovel. Will was aware of disaster before they even reached it. Screams rang around the dirty street and Scrapper raced ahead, barking furiously. Will, with Colonel Foot panting behind, ran as fast as he could to the gap where once there had been a door. A dead Frenchman lay sprawled across it.

Inside was chaos. The children's few belongings were strewn everywhere and the baby was yelling her head off. Juan was lying bleeding from a head wound in a corner while a British soldier, his trousers unbuttoned, was trying to drag Maria onto the floor. Sarah was screaming and trying to pull herself away from a tall, skinny, bare-assed private intent on rape. Two more soldiers were watching and laughing while the baby yelled loudly. Even as

Will and Scrapper burst through the door, Amy Rogers swung the musket Will had left behind and brought it down hard on the head of the man who was now on top of Maria. The soldier grunted and fell to one side. Meanwhile, Will aimed the musket he had found and, at point-blank range, shot in the buttocks the man who was struggling with Sarah, making him yell like a stuck pig. Scrapper leapt on him and mauled him for good measure. The two men who had been watching saw Colonel Foot enter the hovel with his sword drawn, decided that escape was preferable to explanation, and made a run for it. The man Amy had felled came round and tried to get up, but found himself with the point of the Colonel's sword at his throat. Maria pulled down her skirts and ran to kneel by the prostrate Juan.

But where was Megan? Will helped Sarah to her feet. The girl was white with shock. "Where's Megan?" he demanded, his stomach clenching in fear that she was dead. "Where is she?" The girl stared at him uncomprehendingly, seeming not to realise who he was. He caught hold of her arms and shook her. "Sarah! It's me! Will! Where's Megan? Answer me, damn it!"

Sarah blinked several times then her eyes focused on him at last. Her face screwed up as she started to cry softly. "Will!" she said. "Megan's gone. With Deneuve. He's taken her again. It was Carmen. She led him here. Maybe she thought that if Deneuve had Megan he would leave her alone. And I think she wanted to get back at you. We tried to stop him but he had men with him. There were too many." She looked across at Juan. Maria had torn a strip from her skirt and wrapped it around Juan's head to staunch the blood. "Juan threw his knife at him, but got one of his men instead. Deneuve shot him. They'd only just gone when these men came." Tears welled and slid down her cheeks. "Oh, Will! Rosa's gone too! She was scared and ran away. She's out there alone."

Will's insides churned at the thought of little mute Rosa at the mercy of the pillaging British. And he was back to square one as far as Megan was concerned because she had been returned to the clutches of Major Deneuve. Only this time it was worse because Megan had lost all trust in him.

Carmen. He seethed at the thought of her betrayal. He had never before felt the urge to kill a woman, but he knew that if he saw her again, he would have no compunction in ending her life.

Where to start? He forced himself to think about their present situation. The first thing he had to do was to see that the children, Sarah, and Amy were taken out of the city. That's where Colonel Foot would be able to help. He asked the officer if he could see them all to safety. The Colonel willingly agreed. Foot stepped towards Maria, but she cradled her brother closer and said something in a harsh voice in her own language, her look at once defiant.

"It's all right, Maria," said Will gently. "'E's 'ere ter 'elp. 'E won't 'urt yer.'"

Slowly Maria stood up and stepped away from Juan, allowing the officer to examine the boy. He stood up stiffly. "It is little more than a scratch," he said. "The boy will recover but we need transport. He needs a doctor."

"Lightfoot!" said Will immediately. "There's a pony I came 'ere on. 'E's stabled. I'll fetch 'im if 'e's still there."

"Is it far?"

"Near the walls."

"Could be just the thing," said Foot. "But be careful, lad. And don't worry about this lot. I'll stay with 'em," said Foot. "Here." He handed Will a pistol. "It's loaded, and will be less noticeable than that musket. Hurry now, the lad's lost a lot of blood."

The two would-be rapists had used the Colonel's distraction with Juan as an opportunity to escape but he knew that if they survived the night he could easily find them again and mete out suitable punishment. He gave Will some powder and cartridges for the pistol and without further ado, the boy ran out of the house with Scrapper.

Will remembered where he had stabled Lightfoot but it seemed such a long time ago. By himself he was easily able to avoid the British, and even when he encountered groups of drunks, they took no notice of what they assumed to be a penniless peasant boy. He tried to close his mind to the screams and weeping that came from hovels and doorways on his way, intent only on getting the girls and Juan out of the city, and then finding Deneuve, Megan, and Rosa. He watched for the latter two but saw nothing of them.

He found Lightfoot though. The place had been ransacked by the British, the owner dead and bloody on a bed of straw, the only occupants a mule and Lightfoot who had obviously been deemed too old to be of any use. Will could not find a saddle but grabbed a bundle of rope which he tied around the horse's neck as a sort of harness.

Deciding that riding would be quicker, Will scrambled onto the pony's back. It was a hair-raising ride. Gun shots, explosions and screams did not frighten Lightfoot and he ambled along as slowly as if he was on a field trail at home in England, until Will urged him into a gallop. Once he had got going though, there was no stopping him and Will was hard put to stay on the horse as he careened around corners, forcing people out of the way, and knocking some of the more drunken ones aside. However, he made it back to Maria's house without incident.

At first Maria refused to go. "What about Rosa?" she wailed. "I cannot go without Rosa."

"I'll look for 'er, Maria," said Will. "I'll find 'er. Don't worry. Go with the Colonel. You 'ave ter get out of the city! Go now!" He helped the distraught girl onto the pony's broad back behind the Colonel and then lifted Juan to sit in front of the officer. Sarah and Amy were to walk alongside, taking turns to carry the baby.

When they were all set to go, Sarah kissed Will on the cheek. "Take care," she said, her face serious. Will nodded. "You too," he answered.

"Don't you worry, lad. I'll look after them," said Colonel Foot confidently. "Maybe I'll find some men on the way who've still got a modicum of sense, and they can escort us. I hope you find the Captain's niece and the little girl. Look after yourself now."

Will nodded and held up his hand in farewell as the horse and people walked slowly down the street.

Chapter 17

Will stared at the body of the French soldier in the doorway of the hovel and wondered where to go first. Would Deneuve have escaped the city, or was he still here? He thought back to the scene at the breaches. No. Wellington would have seen to it that once the British had taken Badajoz, all exits would be well guarded so that the French could not escape. But Deneuve was a wily man and he would not want to be taken prisoner, his undoubted fate if the British found him. Where would he hide?

The first place to look was the house Deneuve had commandeered, the place where he and Megan had been held captive. Maybe there he would find a clue as to the man's whereabouts, a servant perhaps who would be willing to talk. Will had given Colonel Foot back his pistol, but he had the musket, and Juan's knife that he'd pulled from the body of the dead Frenchman at his feet. He looked around for anything else he might be able to use but there was nothing. The children's few rags of clothing, blankets, and a couple of candles were scattered around the room but there was no food or anything of value at all so he whistled for Scrapper and they set off into the streets once more.

The journey to the large house where Major Deneuve had had his headquarters was fraught with danger. A large proportion of the drunken British soldiers had now formed aggressive groups that roamed the streets looking for trouble. Many were fighting each other. Some with murder on their minds sought out French soldiers from their hiding places and the city still rang to the screams of the dying and the raped. Frightened children peered out of doorways or ran aimlessly, searching for their mothers and safety. Will looked for Rosa but did not see her.

At last he came to the high wall that surrounded the house. This part of the city was relatively quiet and he wondered why until he found the gates and saw that they had been ripped off their hinges. The British had been here already. He hurried up the dark silent driveway, ever watchful for the enemy and men from his own side, but saw no one. The front door was like the gate, hacked to splinters and hanging from one loose hinge. On entering the hallway, he looked around for a light of some sort. Feeling around he found a candle stub but nothing to light it with. Groping around in the dark, he fell over a broken table. Scrapper had wandered off, and then Will heard him barking from another room. With the musket held tightly, Will made for the noise. Scrapper was in the kitchen, and there was a lit oil lamp, still standing on the table.

"Good boy, Scrapper!" said Will, bending down to pat the dog. He picked up the lamp and started to go from room to room, searching for any clue as to Megan's whereabouts but it was very apparent that the house had been ransacked. Glass lay shattered on the floor, furniture was fire-wood, windows had been broken and the previous owners' household belongings flung around with abandon.

A trail of blood spattered on a tiled floor led Will to the first body, that of a French soldier, and he recognised one of Deneuve's men. The French had put up a fight. Furniture was up-turned and there were more bodies, both French and British, in every room on the ground floor. Will surmised that a band of British soldiers had taken the house hoping for plunder and had run into Major Deneuve's Company who were holding it. There seemed to be more French dead than British, but no sign of any prisoners. The house was silent and appeared empty.

Back in the ravaged kitchen, Will righted a wooden chair and sat down to think what to do next. Scrapper was sniffing around but then the dog straightened up, his head to one side, ears pricked, listening intently. "What is it, boy?" Will whispered, suddenly as alert as the dog. Scrapper whined, then padded to a door set in the far wall and growled softly. Will listened. Then he heard it too, a small noise, a scuffle as of soft footsteps. Quietly, he crept to the door. There was a key in the lock. With Juan's knife firmly held in one hand, he slowly turned the key and flung open the door.

Scrapper immediately started barking and the person crouched on the dark steps that led down into a cellar let out a cry of terror. Will, who a few moments before had been expecting to see a soldier, let out the breath he did not know he had been holding, and grabbed Carmen Garcia by her dirty hair, forcing her back against the wall.

"Where is she?" he shouted, his angry face inches from the girl's terrified eyes, the knife in his fist. "Where's Megan?" The sight of the girl sent thoughts of murder racing through his head. Usually he would have had second thoughts about killing, or even hitting a woman, but Carmen had betrayed both himself and Megan. The hand that held the knife to her throat shook with suppressed rage and he knew that just a tiny push would end the girl's life. It was with great difficulty that he resisted the impulse.

"Where is she?" he shouted again, and he pulled Carmen's hair back hard so that her head struck the wall behind her. Scrapper growled from the top of the steps.

Carmen cried out and stared into the eyes so close to hers, trembling with fear but trying to still herself, afraid that the knife blade would cut her throat if she moved too much. She recognised the rage etched on Will's face and knew he would kill her without a second thought if she did not tell him the truth now.

"She is with Deneuve," she said, wincing at the pain he was causing.

"I know that! Where?" Will demanded, pushing her even harder against the wall.

"Let go and I will tell you." Carmen's voice shook. This boy would kill her. She could see it in his eyes.

Slowly, Will let go of her hair and drew the knife away a little, taking a step backwards onto the step above. Carmen pulled herself away from the wall warily, her eyes never leaving his face.

"Men from your army, they come early this morning," she said. "There was a fight. Deneuve hid with your woman and me here, in the cellar. He lock the door. The fight was ended but it was a long time before he open the door. I hear soldiers steal and rape servants. We hear much shouting and crying. He need somewhere to hide from your soldiers so I tell him of cellar in plaza. He take her with him." Carmen's eyes narrowed, and Will saw the hatred in them. "He not take me. I try to get out but he lock the door. I bang but no one hear me." She stared at the broken bodies on the kitchen floor and said sadly, "They all dead." Her eyes, scared, turned to his face. "Please, you will not kill me?"

Every instinct in Will's body told him he should do just that. This girl had caused him and Megan, and her so-called friends, endless trouble and put them in great danger. She had even betrayed her own brother. Who would miss her? No one. And perhaps that's why he couldn't do it. He knew what it was like to be alone and for a tiny moment he pitied her.

That look of pity was his undoing. Carmen saw it. In a trice, the expression on her face changed from beseeching to cunning. Quickly she pulled away from the wall and ducked under his arm. She raced into the kitchen and out of the door.

For a moment Will hesitated, wondering whether it was worth it to follow her, but then he heard Carmen shouting, and her voice cut off by gun-fire.

Scrapper barked again and followed Will as he hefted the musket and ran through the house to a room overlooking the main driveway.

A group of men, one holding a flaming torch, were staring at Carmen's body that lay on the ground. The goulish light showed blood, black and sticky, on her dirty white blouse. Next to her, a drunken British corporal was beating an equally intoxicated private with his fists.

"Yer bloody fool!" shouted the corporal, staggering and swinging wildly. "We could've 'ad her first! D'yer want ter fuck a bloody corpse?"

The two were watched by three more privates, all swaying and bleary eyed. One carried a sack. He shifted its weight on his shoulder but the change made him stagger and stumble over his own feet. This caused one of the others to swear as the sack bumped his hip. In seconds, all five were aiming punches at each other. Will took the fracas as his chance to go. He blew out the lamp, then he and Scrapper ran out of the front door and into the dark shrubbery against the wall. Keeping the bushes between himself and the soldiers, they managed to get away unseen.

Back in the streets where fires cast dark shadows, Will slowed to a walk. He was tired. When had he last slept? He couldn't remember. Neither could he remember when he had eaten but he wasn't hungry. Fear for Megan was the only thing that gnawed at his stomach. As for Carmen, he felt nothing for her. He had hated her, had even thought of killing her himself, and he wondered how he could have been taken in by her feminine whiles. Now she was dead and could do them no more harm.

He came to the cathedral plaza and paused for a moment, the loaded musket in his hand. Smoke billowed up from a fire to one side of the big building and he had a sense of déjà vu. It reminded him of the church where he had seen Juanita die in Ciudad Rodrigo. There the church had been lit by a fire in the street behind, but this seemed closer, possibly even from the cathedral itself. Suddenly men appeared, British soldiers running. The fire-light glinted from a gold cross, chalices, and candle sticks. Will did not think to try and stop them. He supposed it was wrong to rob a church, but there was a time when he might have done it himself to keep from starving.

He crept stealthily towards the ornate building that housed the cellar. It appeared empty as it had ever since his arrival in Badajoz. Nevertheless, he took care not to be seen from the windows. The plaza was now deserted too, the soldiers gone with their spoils, but then he heard shouts and raucous singing. Not wanting to be seen he kept to the darker shadows and ran to the top of the cellar steps, then paused when he heard voices from below.

Will sidled down the steps keeping close to the wall, and a voice he recognised floated up from the gloom.

"You will come to like me, *cherie*. When the war is won and we are in Paris, I will buy you silken gowns and a necklace of pearls to put around your pretty neck." Deneuve's voice was wheedling, as smooth as the gowns he was promising to buy. Will took another step, musket at the ready,

"Never!" This was shouted, and Will's heart leapt. It was Megan, but then the invective that followed was suddenly cut off by a strangled cry. Will ran down the last two steps, through the short dark tunnel and into the semi-darkness of the cellar.

A guttering candle lit up Major Deneuve and Megan, while huge shadows played out the scene on the wall behind them. The Frenchman's hand was around the girl's throat, under her chin, pushing her backwards. Megan's bodice was torn, her breasts exposed. Deneuve was cursing in French, his other hand up her skirt while she struggled to get away.

The shot that rang out echoed around the cellar, deafening two of the occupants. The third fell to the floor and lay still.

Crying with relief, and all thoughts of his earlier betrayal with Carmen flying from her head, Megan ran to Will, who did not wait to see if the sound of the gunshot would bring anyone to investigate. He grabbed her hand and ran with her out of the cellar and into the plaza. A group of men, soldiers dressed in gaudy scraps of civilian clothing, were breaking into buildings to the right, across the cobbles. There was the sound of breaking glass, and shouts from inside the wrecked doorways. Megan ignored them and wrapped her arms around Will's neck. Fiercely, he hugged her back while Scrapper barked at them and wagged his tail, seemingly pleased to see them together again. They stood like that for several moments, then Megan lifted her face to be kissed.

Will felt relief, and something else. Standing in the plaza, lit by the flames from the cathedral but with the air stinking from smoke and rancid with death and destruction, he knew more than anything else that he loved this girl, and that he never wanted to let her go. He wanted to love her, not just with all his heart, but physically. He manouvered her into the darker shadows under the covered walkway, and his hand moved towards her bare breast, but then Megan seemed to become aware of his feelings because she shivered and pulled away. She dropped her hands from around his neck and Scrapper licked one of them.

Will took a deep breath and looked at Megan properly for the first time since entering the cellar. She was thinner and dirty, her once gleaming hair matted and lank. Her clothes were rags and her face was streaked with tears and strained. She was still crying. "Oh, Megan," he said softly, and gathered her in his arms again, his lusty thoughts of a moment before dying quickly as he realised how distressed she was. Remembering their last meeting, he wondered how he could have been so stupid as to let Carmen seduce him. "I'm sorry," he said. "Really sorry. About Carmen," he added, in case she wondered what he was talking about. "I was an idiot. I love yer. Please forgive me." Megan said nothing. She would forgive him, of course she would. Hadn't he come to her rescue yet again? But it was really hard, knowing that other girls wanted him as much as she did. She listened again as he spoke, his voice muffled slightly by her hair as she clung to him.

"Did Deneuve do anythin' to yer?"

"No," she said, her small voice even more so, speaking as she was into his shirt. "He wanted me as a trophy. He talked all the time about what he was going to do with me when he was back in France. I just kept quiet and let him rant on." She stopped and looked up into his face, the face that she loved so dearly. "Then I couldn't stand it any more, and …" A tear trickled down her cheek. "You came just in time."

Will nodded, trying not to think what would have happened if he had been just a few minutes later. God! How was he to keep Megan from being raped? This was the second time he had managed to save her, but all the time she was so attractive to men, and in such a dangerous place, there would always be that danger. What if next time he was too late? There was only one solution.

"Marry me," he said.

"What?"

"Marry me. And go 'ome. 'Ome ter Camberwell 'All. It's not safe for yer 'ere."

Megan's expression changed instantly to one of anger. She stepped away from him, drawing the tattered edges of her bodice together to hide her breasts.

"I can't believe you said that, Will Tucker!" she exclaimed loudly.

"What did I say?" said Will, bewildered by her sudden change of mood.

"That! Telling me to go home! After everything I went through to get here and stay here, despite Uncle Richard forever trying his best to get me on the next ship back to England! How could you even think I would want to go?"

"I thought … after this …" Will was stuck for words. He shook his head.

Women. He would never understand them. Then he grinned suddenly as a thought struck him.

"Yer may not want ter go 'ome," he said, his eyes twinkling. "But yer never said yer didn't want ter marry me."

Megan's anger evaporated as quickly as it had come. She blushed and put her arms around him again. "Of course I want to marry you," she said, then she scowled. "If only to keep other girls from wanting to bed you!" Now it was Will's turn to blush scarlet. Then Megan sighed deeply. "But Uncle will never allow it. Not yet anyway."

"Why not?" Will's voice rose with anger. Did Richard Camberwell think he wasn't good enough for his niece?

"It's not what you think, silly," said Megan, reading his mind. "He knows I want to marry you, but he would rather we waited until the war is over."

"But that might take years!" Will protested. "Besides, it's fer yer own good! If yer wore a ring, it might make bastards like 'im keep 'is 'ands ter 'imself." He nodded his head back towards the cellar.

Megan doubted that in wartime anything would keep men like Major Deneuve from taking exactly what, and whoever, they wanted. And the evidence that nearly every soldier thought the same was all around them. Even Will, who professed to love her, had his moments when he behaved like every other soldier far from home.

"It won't," she said sadly. "And I do want to marry you, Will. Very much. But for now I want to keep in Uncle's good books or he'll make me go home. Maybe if the war carries on, he'll change his mind."

Megan said the noble words but looking into Will's handsome face, her thoughts were off on an entirely different track. She had not missed the few seconds when he had wanted to make love to her. It had happened before. The hardness of him as he pressed her to him, that sudden ardour in his kiss. The trouble was, she knew she wanted him too. She felt a delicious thrill creeping up from her toes every time she thought of him. The way his hair curled around the back of his neck, and the sight of his strong, brown forearms made her go all funny. Every time he held her, she wanted his touch to last forever. Was it normal to feel like that for a man? She supposed it was. She had learned much about what girls thought of the opposite sex since coming to the Peninsula and mixing with the women who followed the army. Although their talk about men was often crude and lewd, they had taught her a lot about what it was like to love a man, and Megan knew she loved Will. And since she had found out about Carmen, the forbidden thought had also crossed her mind that if she gave herself to him, it might stop him feeling the need to do "things" with other girls. Innocent as she was, she pushed the thought away as unworthy, yet it kept coming back. It was a problem.

A problem she could no longer ponder on, for at that moment there was a mighty explosion that made them both jump, and Scrapper start barking madly again.

The fire that the British had started when they had plundered the cathedral had spread, and it seemed that the French had used the church as another gunpowder store. Explosions sent gouts of flame and showers of stone up into the air and across the cobbles of the plaza.

"Come on!" Will shouted over the thunderous noise and pulled Megan after him towards the shelter of buildings further away as pieces of stone and wood rained down around them. Then Megan, looking backwards at the cathedral, screamed and yanked on his hand. "Stop, Will! It's Rosa!"

Will turned and there was little Rosa running from the direction of the church. "Oh, God, Will! She'll be killed!" Megan started to run after her, but Will pushed her back roughly.

"No! Go there!" He shouted, pointing to buildings on the other side. "Away from those soldiers! Yer'll be safer there! I'll get 'er!" Without waiting to see if she obeyed him, he ran back the way they had come. Scrapper had also seen Rosa and was bounding towards her, ignoring the falling debris and the flames that shot up into the air.

"Rosa!" Will shouted, but the little girl gave no sign that she had heard him. She ran through a broken doorway. Will followed, still calling her name, Scrapper at his side. Then there was another huge bang and the world exploded.

Chapter 18

Will coughed until he imagined he had no lungs left. Dust hung like fog in the air and it was hard to breathe. He was on his back and there was a heavy weight on his legs. He reached out through the swirling dust particles and his fingers touched fur. Scrapper. The dog was lying next to him, and quivered under his touch, whimpering softly. Will tried to remember where he was, then it came to him. Rosa. Where was she? He lifted his head and bits of masonry dropped from his hair. There was a huge hole in the ceiling where the floor above had fallen through. Stones, planks of wood, and broken furniture loomed out of the dust. What if the rest of the building should fall? They would be buried alive. It was a thought he dismissed almost as soon as it occurred to him. It was too awful to contemplate. He cast his eyes about the room. There was Rosa. She was sitting in the middle of a pile of stone, her eyes wide and frightened, staring at him, but seeming miraculously unhurt.

Will smiled at her reassuringly, but then looked up sharply when there was an ominous creak from above and more dust filtered through the hole in the ceiling. They had to get out. He tried to move his legs, and grimaced as pain shot up the right one. Damn! Was it broken? He pushed at the block of masonry and wooden planks that covered it. The rubble moved a little, so he pushed harder. Nothing happened. Try something else. With his hands he managed to remove the wood that covered his other leg and then pushed hard at the biggest stone with his foot. Sweating with exertion he used all his strength and the stone and wood shifted enough for him to pull his leg out. From the knee down was lacerated and bloody. No wonder. He could see nails sticking out of the planks. Some of them had scraped down his leg. Not broken then, thank God. He pushed away some other rubble and found he could kneel, though he almost screamed at the pain in his right leg. He saw the musket lying nearby and picked it up. The stock was scratched and he blew away the dust but the weapon seemed usable.

Scrapper was whining but his tail was wagging and he raised his head to look at Will.

"Good boy!" said Will, relieved that he was all right. He stroked the dog and then crawled slowly towards Rosa who sat as though frozen. When he reached her, he cradled her in his arms.

"It's all right, Rosa! I've got yer. We'll get out of 'ere, don't yer worry," he said, trying to comfort the little girl who suddenly started to shake with shock. "Come on. Come with me."

Rosa shook her head, her eyes terrified. "It's all right. We'll be fine," said Will. "Come on now." He tried to move her, but Rosa made a small mewing sound and shook her head again, pulling away from him. Will glanced up at the ceiling as it creaked again. The whole lot could come down at any minute. They had to get out.

Scrapper, lying in the dust, watched Will's efforts, then slithered on his stomach through the debris towards them. Rosa's eyes seemed to focus on the dog and she laid a hand on his fur, then clutched it tightly. Will smiled at the dog, realising what the intelligent animal was doing.

"That's right,' he said to Rosa. "You 'old on ter Scrapper, and we'll soon have yer out of 'ere."

There wasn't room for Scrapper to turn around, so the dog edged backwards with Rosa clinging like a limpet to his back, until he came to a clearer space where he could turn and go forwards, crawling under and around the obstacles. Will crawled too, trying to ignore the pain in his leg. He carried the musket in one hand, unwilling to leave it behind.

A lighter patch showed where the doorway had been but it was partially blocked with fallen masonry and wood. "Will! Will!" Megan's voice from outside wafted through the dusty air. "Will! Are you all right?"

He called back, and then heard other voices and saw stones being moved. People were clearing away the rubble. The patch of early dawn grew rapidly bigger.

"Be careful!" he shouted. "The 'ole lot's about ter come down!"

Even as he said it, there was a rumbling sound from behind and above. "Move!" he shouted to the dog, pushing its rump hard. Scrapper scrabbled on loose stones, then he and Rosa emerged into fresh air, willing hands pulling them the last few yards. Will saw Megan's worried face outlined against the lightening sky, then a hand grabbed his and he was pulled free. He was helped to his feet and limped and hobbled away, just as what was left of the building tumbled down in a crashing, dusty heap behind them.

Coughing again, Will fell to his hands and knees until he felt Megan's arms around him. She was saying something but he couldn't quite take it in, then a different voice penetrated his consciousness and he heard Megan's sharp intake of breath.

"So, we meet yet again." The voice was cold, calculating, but overlaid by something else. Pain. Will looked up. Major Deneuve was only a few steps away, a pistol in his hand. He was dishevelled, without his shako, his uniform torn and dusty, and there was a big bloody smear congealed on the left shoulder of his jacket. Will's heart sank. Why had he not stayed in the cellar long enough to make sure the man was dead? It could well prove the costliest mistake of his life. Slowly, gasping at the pain in his leg, he stood up.

Two soldiers stood close by, the men who had helped get them out of the ruined building, but they were without weapons. By their uniforms, they were British privates. One started to say something angrily to Deneuve, but the other pulled at his sleeve and shook his head. Both edged warily away. Deneuve took not the slightest notice, only interested in Will and Megan. Once behind him and out of his sight, the two men ran.

"You thought I was dead," said Deneuve. "But, as you see, I am very much alive." His eyes flickered over Megan who stood next to Will. "Come here, *ma cherie,*" he said. Megan did not move.

"She's not goin' with yer!" Will said through clenched teeth, and he brought the musket up until it was level with Deneuve's stomach. The Frenchman's lips smiled, though his eyes glared hatred, the flames from the cathedral lighting his back. Suddenly, he reached out and grabbed Rosa who was closer. The girl screamed and shouted, "Will!"

"Now. We will do a trade," said Deneuve nastily. "Your girl for this one. If you do not do as I say, I will kill her." To make his point, the Frenchman dug the pistol into the child's ribs, making her scream again. Deneuve held her tightly in front of him, effectively cutting off any attempt Will might make to use the musket.

Realising with shock that Rosa had called his name, Will knew the situation was desperate. What could he do? For seconds no one moved, then there was a sudden blur of fur and a feral growl that came from deep within Scrapper's very soul. The dog leapt at Deneuve. His teeth sank into the man's neck, Rosa squirmed free, and the pistol went off.

Deneuve went down with Scrapper on top of him. Rosa ran to Will and Megan, calling their names. Megan caught her and hugged her close.

Suddenly all that could be heard was the crackle of flames from the burning cathedral. Slowly, very slowly, Will limped towards the man and the dog, still on the ground.

He knelt awkwardly beside them. He saw immediately that Deneuve was dead, his throat opened up by Scrapper's teeth, the blood running thick on his neck and torn jacket. Scrapper was alive but there was a big red hole in his chest where the pistol's bullet had entered, the blood wetting Deneuve's clothes and mingling with that of the Frenchman.

As gently as he could, Will lifted the dog away from Deneuve's body. Scrapper looked up at him. His expression was both puzzled and imploring, as though he didn't know what was happening to him and expected Will to do something to help.

"Oh, no, Scrapper! Don't die! Please don't die!" Will whispered, tears streaming down his face. He sat on the cobbles and stroked the dog's silky head. The scared, painful look in Scrapper's big brown eyes was one Will would never forget and would always make him feel terrible when he thought about it, because he knew there was nothing he could do. The wound was mortal and the dog was dying.

Scrapper licked Will's hand and he whimpered. His chest moved spasmodically up and down, the breath rasping in his throat. How long they sat like that, Will had no idea, but gradually the light faded from Scrapper's eyes, his breathing slowed even more until it finally stopped, and his head sank further onto Will's lap. Will looked up through his tears to see that Megan was standing beside them with one arm around Rosa, the other hand covering her lips, and they were crying too. Raindrops spattered them as the sky grew gradually lighter.

They heard a shout and Will slowly turned his head to see soldiers running towards them from one of the alleys that led into the plaza. Through eyes swimming with tears, he registered Ron Parker's bulk and Nat Binns's bow-legged run, and then Richard Camberwell riding on Hades.

After that everything was a blur. He, Megan, and Rosa were taken out of Badajoz and back to the British camp. His leg was found not to be broken, just badly lacerated and bruised. Rosa was reunited with her siblings and the next thing Will remembered clearly was waking up the next morning, lying on Captain Camberwell's camp cot, with Megan telling him to drink the cup of tea she had in her hand.

"It's real tea, Will," she said. "Mrs. Dutton gave it to me for you. Said she was saving it for a special occasion and that you deserve it." She smiled and Will smiled back, glad to see her fairly clean and looking more like her old self again. She chattered away as he drank the tea, thinking he had never tasted anything so good.

"The women say you're a real hero, going off to rescue Sarah, Amy, and me like that," she said. "And everyone's so pleased that Rosa can talk again. The surgeon thinks there was nothing physically wrong with her, it was the trauma of losing her parents. Another shock brought her voice back. Oh, and by the way, George wants to see you. He's still bed-ridden but much better and they've managed to save his arm, and I heard that Wellington himself wants to speak with you too, as soon as it's convenient."

"Well, it's not convenient yet," said Will, grimly, tossing back the blanket as a bad memory returned with a jolt. "There's something I 'ave ter do first."

Megan nodded slowly. She had guessed what he had in mind. "He's here. Beside the tent," she said quietly, her liveliness draining away in a second and her eyes filling with tears again. "Ron and Nat wanted to bury him but I told them not to. I knew you'd want to do it yourself."

Will gave her a forlorn smile and kissed her on the lips. "Thank you," he said.

*

Sir Arthur Wellesley, Viscount Wellington, watched from a hillside as Will Tucker patted the earth down on top of Scrapper's grave, then dropped the spade and put his arm around Lady Megan Camberwell. Beside them stood Rosa and Juan, Sarah and Amy, with Maria carrying the baby.

"A grave for a dog," commented Wellington drily. "It's more than some soldiers get, Richard."

"It is, sir," agreed Camberwell quietly. "But, in this case, well deserved, I think."

"Just so, Captain. Just so," agreed Wellington, nodding his head sagely. There was a pause and then, "It seems that lad of yours is making quite a name for himself. I might even need to promote him one day."

Richard Camberwell knew it was most unlikely that Will would ever be anything but a lowly private. Promotion from the ranks was almost impossible to achieve in the British army. Still, you never knew what could happen in wartime. There might yet come a day when he would be talking to his servant as an equal. Despite the sombre scene in front of him, he smiled at the thought.

*

That evening, Will walked alone to the top of the same hill that overlooked

Badajoz. Hazy smoke swirled into the grey clouds that hung over the city, but it had rained and most of the fires were now out. There was still trouble inside the walls, but Wellington was threatening to hang the worst offenders and officers were slowly gaining the upper hand. Soldiers still swarmed over the breaches, but these were carrying away the bodies. Others, closer, used the trenches they had dug, as graves. Will looked away to a solitary one he, Nat, and Ron had dug that afternoon. Bob Tomkins had been laid to rest there, with Molly and her family weeping tears of grief that brought a lump to his throat when he thought of it.

The lump got bigger when he stared at the bottom of the hill. There was another grave, topped by a crude wooden cross. He had burned the words into it himself – 'Scrapper, a friend and hero.' Tears started to fall again, and he roughly brushed them away.

He heard his name called and looked behind him to see Sergeant Readman puffing his way up the hillside towards him. When he finally reached the top, Readman paused for a few moments to get his breath back.

"At last!" he complained eventually. "Had plenty people lookin' for you, my lad, and Wellington's seethin'. Expected you in 'is tent an hour ago, 'e did! Didn't you get the message?"

Will shrugged. Wellington might be the army's commander but sometimes there were more important things than orders. He had been digging Bob's grave when the message came. He said nothing for a minute or two, then, "It's been a bad couple of days, eh, Sarge?"

"Aye, it has that, lad." Readman had heard the stories. It didn't take long for tales to get around. This lad had been spared the horror of the breaches but had had his own share of hardships. However, Readman was an optimistic fellow. "Every day's a bad day for us soldiers," he said. "This is a day like any other, lad. Anyway, you'd best go and get cleaned up and hurry to the General or you might not see another! Come on now!" And with that, he started back down the hillside.

Sighing deeply, Will reluctantly followed, thinking about what the sergeant had said. He supposed it was a soldier's lot to battle enemies, suffer bad food, awful weather, lack of sleep, and lose good friends. Yet it wasn't all bad. There was comradeship too. And for him there was Megan. Especially Megan.

He paused as he passed Scrapper's grave and the tears threatened to fall again. "Goodbye, my friend," he whispered. "I'll always remember you."

One more good friend lost. Yes, it was just another day.

Historical Note

Badajoz in northern Spain was such a difficult place to besiege, that if it was not thought completely necessary, it is very doubtful that anyone would have ever contemplated trying to do so. Yet Wellington had two tries at it, knowing that if he did not gain the city, then he might as well go home. Judging by the maps of the time, the city could not have been better fortified and one can only imagine the despair and incredulity that must have run through the minds of the British soldiers faced with its bastions for the first time. Not only were those bastions built into the city walls, but there were outlying forts as well which had to be overcome, together with the castle to the north. It was certainly a formidable stronghold, and Ciudad Rodrigo was child's play in comparison.

The French garrison at Badajoz consisted of nearly five thousand men under General Phillipon, and they did everything they could to make things even more difficult for the British attack. They laid mines, deepened ditches and filled them with water, or wood that could be set alight, strengthened the walls and constructed rows of bristling sword blades. The walls themselves, especially at the castle, were so high that the French must have thought that no one would be foolish enough to attempt to climb them but they reckoned without Wellington and the courage of the men who fought under him.

Badajoz is probably the only place in the whole Peninsula where Wellington considered giving up a fight. He had already been defeated once by the city's defences, in June 1811, and he was prepared to be again before Generals Leith and Picton managed to gain a foothold. It is also a matter of record that he was moved to tears when he stood at the breaches after the battle was over and saw the terrible destruction of over three thousand men.

Despite its historical background, this is a work of fiction, and there are several instances where I have used an author's literary licence to help Wellington in his endeavours and to move the story along. There was no reinforcing battalion of French troops ahead of the British when they were on their way from Ciudad Rodrigo. Marshall Soult and the French army were many miles away, as were other French troops, though Wellington did want to hurry the seige, not wanting them to have time to come to the city's aid.

Ammunition and stores were kept in the castle, luckily for Will who could help General Picton when the time was right. As it happened, General Picton's forces needed no help from anyone inside the city, and achieved the amazing feat of scaling the walls and infiltrating the castle by themselves, though with appalling loss of life. The castle was still standing when he did so, as no one set off a four-pound cannon to bring down some of the inner walls and cause confusion amongst the French defenders.

It is quite possible that there were children abandoned in the city under French rule. When the French took over Badajoz, many people left, but others would have stayed and some would have been killed if they had not co-operated with the French. Thus I have made Maria and her brother and sisters orphans of war and given Will friends in his hunt for Megan.

Dogs proved many a soldier's friend in war-time and the army was home to plenty of them. It would be comforting to think that some were as brave as Scrapper and became faithful companions to home-sick soldiers in this violent period of history.

Bibliography

Wellington at War in the Peninsula-An Overview and Guide-1808-1814, by Ian C. Robertson, Lee Cooper - Pen and Sword Books

The Great Duke by Arthur Bryant - Collins Publishers

The Age of Elegance by Arthur Bryant - The Reprint Society by arrangement with Collins

Wellington by Elizabeth Longford - Sutton Publishing

Dictionary of the Napoleonic Wars by Stephen Pope - Facts on File Inc